By

JULIE MATERN

This is a work of historical fiction. Though some of the incidents are based on real events, most of the characters, names, incidents, places, and dialogue are products of the author's imagination and are not to be construed as real.

The opinions and views expressed herein belong solely to the author and do not necessarily represent the opinions or views of Wild Poppy Publishing, LLC. Permission for the use of sources, graphics, and photos is also solely the responsibility of the author.

Published by Wild Poppy Publishing, LLC.
Utah 84003

Cover Design by Julie Matern

Edited by Jolene Perry

She is an over-educated bluestocking who has never met a debate she did not like. He is the boy next door. Will she realize the perfect man is right in front of her?

Olivia is the oldest of the four, beautiful Deverell sisters. She is also a reformed tomboy whose best friend is the earl next door. But she has reached the age where she is expected to marry—and her sisters can't 'come out' until she does. Philosophy, politics and debate of any subject are the tools of her trade but these might not get her far among the social elite of London.

With little enthusiasm for her season, she has a change of heart when she learns that an eminent young scientist will also be in town. Orchestrating events to meet him, she is surprised when he invites her to help him with his work.

Could this be a match made in heaven?

Olivia is Book 1 in the Women of Worcester series.

Dedicated to Gwendoline Alice Ayres Windell

Table of Contents

Prologue

Olivia Deverell was in trouble.

She had missed her footing as she climbed down from the great oak tree and now her ankle was throbbing. She had told Jeremy Worthington that it did not hurt, which was a lie, but she did not want to admit as much to him.

They had climbed higher than usual. He had dared her. She was eleven and could not ignore a dare. It was against all her principles. She had climbed with ease, like her black cat, and her cheeks had almost burst with accomplishment as they sat, higher than ever before, watching the squirrels chase along the gnarled branches. The view from that height was infinitely better.

When it was time to leave, she had been over-confident and climbed down with less caution than usual. That is how it came to pass that half-way down she had not been careful to make her foot sure before descending farther. Her impractical, flat shoe had slipped from the sturdy, familiar branch and she had landed badly. Her cat would have made no such error.

As the wind and branches rushed past her, twigs scratching at her face, she had a moment of regret. But that view! If she had the chance to do it again, she would.

Pain shot through her foot and up her leg and she bit her lip hard to prevent herself from crying out. As she sat, waiting upon Jeremy, an unpleasant pulsing flared with every beat of her guilty heart.

"Are you alright?" His anxious, blue eyes stood out from his summer-freckled nose.

"Of course, I'm alright!" she declared with as much vigor as she could muster, but she could tell from his quirked brow that he was not fooled.

"You fell from a great height," he remarked. "Let me help you home."

"Absolutely not! You will be late for tea. Hurry home now!" She willed herself not to cry.

He squatted in front of her, peering into her dishonest eyes for truth. "Are you sure? I will gladly incur Mother's wrath."

"Jeremy Worthington. Perhaps you did not hear me. I said that I am perfectly fine. I shall rest a little and then be on my way, healthy and whole. I do not need your help, thank you."

Hurt pierced his compassionate features as he unfolded his gangly, twelve-year-old body. "If you insist."

She looked straight ahead avoiding his eye. She would not be able to stay the tears for much longer. "I do."

"I'll see you tomorrow, then."

"Yes, tomorrow." Though she knew that was unlikely.

Jeremy slapped his battered hat onto his unruly, brown curls and began the long walk home, looking back every few yards.

Olivia turned her head away as big, fat tears rolled down her flushed face. She felt her ankle and immediately noticed that the skin was swelling.

As soon as Jeremy was out of sight, she grabbed the rough bark of the oak and pulled herself up, gingerly putting weight on the injured limb. Sharp pain radiated and the tears began to flow fast and free.

Retrieving her forgotten bonnet, she started for home. Limping, every step was agony and she made slow progress. She would completely miss tea and Nanny would report the fact to Mother.

With sheer grit and determination, Olivia hobbled home, entered through the back entrance, and up the stairs to the governess's room.

She knocked.

"Come in!" commanded Miss Kettering.

Olivia pushed open the door and fell into the room, crumpling to the floor.

The governess rushed forward. "Olivia! What have you done this time?"

"I fell from the great oak," she sobbed.

"The very tree your mother forbade you to climb?"

"The very one. Yes."

The kind young woman helped her to a chair and Olivia raised her skirts. Miss Kettering pulled down the stocking to reveal an angry, apple-sized, purple bruise.

She let out an involuntary gasp.

"Is it very bad?" asked Olivia trying to see over her skirts and petticoats.

Miss Kettering placed her cold hands on the ankle and tried to move it, but Olivia cried out in pain.

"I think we should call for the doctor."

"No!" cried Olivia. "Mother said if I got into any more trouble, I would be punished by being kept indoors. I could not bear that, Miss Kettering. Can't you simply bind it with a bandage?"

Miss Kettering chewed the inside of her cheek, contemplating the damage. "It is against my better judgement, Miss Deverell," she began. "But if you will swear not to implicate me in the subterfuge, I will bind your foot."

"Thank you!" Olivia breathed out. "Thank you."

O livia slammed the ancient philosophy book shut, dropped it to the parquet floor and swiftly kicked it under the reading table at the sound of footsteps outside the library door. She grabbed the French verb text and pretended to read, noticing, as the door swung open, that it was upside down.

She quickly righted it.

"Oh, it's just you!" she exclaimed, loosening her grip on the French grammar book as her sister Julia entered, dressed to perfection as usual, not a hair out of place.

"Well, that's not a very nice greeting," retorted her younger sister with a smile. "I take it you were wandering into tomes unsanctioned…again!"

Olivia threw her arms into the air. "Do you know how many science and philosophy books Father possesses that sit here merely gathering dust?" she cried. "It is nigh on heresy to ignore such bounties of knowledge as this."

Julia's lips puckered. "Mother would call it heresy for the daughter of a gentleman to delve into such masculine topics."

"Why couldn't I have been born a boy?" said Olivia, her bodice almost bursting from a deep breath of frustration. "Why should such topics be withheld from me merely because of my sex?"

Pulling out another chair, Julia laid a hand on her sister's taut shoulder. "Because a man is not looking for a wife to argue with him, dearest."

Olivia jutted out her bottom lip and blew another breath through her blondish hair. "Surely they don't want empty mannequins for wives. How dull that would be." She grabbed the fabric of the front of her own dress. "I yearn for knowledge, thirst for it like a stranded man in the desert."

"I know, I know!" declared Julia, lifting her hands as if in defense. "I have not been your sister all these years without being well aware of your opinion on every matter known to man. Frankly, I am surprised there is any room left in your brain for one more iota of facts."

Olivia bent to retrieve the philosophy book, checking that it had not been damaged in the fall. "That is the beauty of the human brain, dear sister. It grows exponentially with every new fact that is placed into it."

"Then you had better beware that your cranium does not crack." Julia stood up. "I came to find an atlas. The governess sent me to get one for Felicity. She failed to identify the major rivers of England this morning and her punishment is to read and study the atlas this afternoon instead of attending her painting lesson."

Olivia found the page she had been reading before the interruption. "A punishment for *her* indeed! As for me, it would be no punishment—I hate to paint and have never improved. I consider it a complete waste of time." She held the forbidden book aloft in triumph. "Did you know that Descartes was—"

Julia interrupted, holding up a finger. "I have no interest in Descartes, Olivia. I confine my own studies to my music and art these days. I am very glad that the days of mathematics and English grammar are behind me."

"But you still enjoy debating on politics, I hope," said Olivia, lowering the book.

Julia sighed. "Debating you is not for the cowardly, but yes, I still enjoy it in small doses. But I fear that as you are going to London for the season, we will need to warn any suitor of yours of your propensity for argument."

A curl had escaped its bounds and Olivia pushed it back behind her ear. "For shame! There is a great deal of difference between argument and debate, Julia. Debate is controlled, considered, linguistic ballet. Argument is much less ordered."

"Then why do I often feel that you are arguing with me in your so-called debates?" Julia had found an atlas. Her other hand she placed on her hip.

"Because I always win!" declared Olivia.

"That may be true, but have you considered the possibility that you merely bludgeon opponents into submission with the force of your passion?" Julia moved toward the door. "I pity the man who puts a ring on your finger."

Olivia's lips jutted out. "Husbands! That is all mother ever speaks of."

"Of course it is! You are twenty-one and not yet married. Mother despairs of you! Which is why she is taking you to London. Do you know how lucky you are? I am already dreaming of my season next year. And besides, it would not be proper for *me* to marry before you, so you had better find yourself a suitable man as I am anxious to start the process." She clasped the large book to her chest and twirled.

Once again finding her place in the forbidden book, Olivia murmured, "I wish you were going instead of me. What use have I for a husband?"

Julia stopped mid-twirl. "Do you not want to have your own home and children? There is no other way."

The book in her hand tipped back, touching the table, as she considered her sister's question. "I don't want a husband who expects me to dress like a doll and keep quiet, no!"

"Then you should marry Jeremy, for I don't wonder that all other men would expect just that."

"Jeremy?" Olivia shook her head, her face lined with disagreement. "Jeremy is my friend! My best friend. I cannot marry a friend. It would spoil everything."

6

Olivia turned in the chair and pulled a newspaper toward her. "There *is* a man," she said, pointing at the print, "who piques my interest. A renowned scientist who is recognized by the Royal Society. Stephen Manwaring. He is a great adventurer and gives lectures on science and the like. He will be in London on a speaking tour when I am there for my season. I just have to figure out how to convince Mama to take me to one of his lectures. I am sure if I can only be introduced to him, I can prove my intelligence. I wager we would find we have a lot in common."

Julia huffed. "And how old is this man?"

"I don't know." She looked at her sister with defiance. "It matters not to me how old he is if he would only be the kind of husband that would let me read and study and share in his work."

"But what if he is as old as Father? Or older? Imagine if he has rheumatism and grey whiskers or walks with a stick?"

Olivia glanced at the lame foot hidden under her gown.

"Oh, forgive me!" cried Julia. "How insensitive. But you hardly limp anymore. I am sure that no one will notice."

"It only bothers me when I walk a long way or dance too long. And sometimes when there is a storm. I hope that a man of letters would overlook my impairment." She replaced the newspaper on the tabletop.

"Any man that would hold such a thing against you is not worthy." Julia's cheeks colored as anger spiked in her blood.

Another girl entered the library. She was tall and willowy, her rich, auburn hair braided around her head. Everyone accepted that she was the most beautiful of the four sisters. "Julia!" cried Genevieve. "Miss Crow sent me to fetch you. She is waiting for the atlas you were commissioned to find." Olivia admired how the green of her dress matched the green of her eyes.

7

Julia's hand flew to her cheek as she checked the ornate clock on the mantle. "Oh my! I'd best away." She ran gracefully from the room.

Genevieve Deverell came to sit by Olivia. Her playful eyes danced with mischief. "And what are *you* doing, big sister?"

Olivia held up the book. "Discovering the wonders of Descartes."

A beautiful sound like the burbling of the brook on their property escaped her sister's peachy lips. "I should not put 'wonders' in a sentence with 'Descartes' myself. But I admire that he invigorates your mind, so." She walked over to the window and looked out at the lawn that stretched to the little forest. Turning she said, "I must warn you; Mother is looking for you."

Olivia chuckled. "She merely wants to talk to me of fittings for dresses and London manners. I have been hiding from her in here all morning."

"Well, she is in a fine temper now," responded Genevieve. "You had better emerge from your hiding place rather than subject us all to her fury." She made a shooing motion. "Go along!"

Olivia replaced the philosophy book under the table so that she might find it easily, and reluctantly left the library with Genevieve trailing her.

"When mother is done with you, I should like your opinion on the poor baskets I have made up. I noticed that Willy Simpkins had no shoes last week and with all the rain we've been having I should like to ensure that all the children on the estate will be shod."

"If I survive my etiquette lesson, I shall look for you," Olivia replied. She loved her generous sister's charitable inclinations but had less affection for being commandeered into helping with all of them.

Genevieve bounced away holding her hand high. "I shall expect you before tea."

8

Rounding the corridor, Olivia pushed into her mother's parlor.

"There you are! I have been searching for you these thirty minutes. Where have you been?" Mrs. Deverell's round face was still beautiful and devoid of wrinkles, though Olivia suspected that she might be the cause of some in the near future.

"I uh, well—"

"Never mind that now," cried her mother. "Come, come. The dressmaker has arrived."

Though Olivia was not immune to the enticement of new dresses, being fitted for them was quite another matter. She could think of little else she would be less inclined to spend the afternoon doing.

Chapter 2
Jeremy

Jeremy Worthington, Earl of Barclay, stood, hand on the window frame, his gaze in the direction of Deverell House. His gaze often drifted that way. His inclination was to ride over, but he had pressing matters to discuss with his agent.

He could hear his mother talking to her companion, Mrs. Robinson, in the next room. He wished, as he had often done, that his mother could have had a daughter to provide her with companionship but alas, she was a sickly woman who had almost died giving birth to him.

"Jeremy!" she cried, the lace on her cap trembling, as he walked into the room. He stooped to give her a kiss on the cheek. "I was just telling Mrs. Robinson that I thought I saw a bud on the cherry trees."

As an invalid, Jeremy's mother sat reclining for most of the day, only able to undertake sedentary tasks such as needle work and reading. Her interests were severely narrowed by her circumstances and Jeremy struggled against finding her company tiresome.

"I can attest to the same conclusion, Mother. Only yesterday I mentioned the same thing to Jackson, the gardener."

The Dowager Countess of Barclay flicked her lacy handkerchief, keeping her eyes trained on the window. "Now, if we could only fill the garden with grandchildren."

Jeremy sighed.

Almost every day his mother said a similar thing, cutting him to the heart. He knew it was his duty to marry and produce an heir. And grandchildren would be a welcome distraction for his sickly mother, but the only girl he could ever imagine filling that role had made it clear that she did not consider him husband material.

"I hope you will be going up for the London season after Easter," his mother continued. "I hate to see you so lonely."

"I am not lonely, Mother. I have you and the Deverells to keep me company. I want for nothing more. But I will go if it pleases you."

Ever since Olivia had told him that her mother insisted that she do a season in town, Jeremy had made plans to stay at his townhome in London. Why he felt the need to torture himself by watching her do the rounds he did not know, but he *did* know that he was powerless to stay away.

He had loved her with a childish love when they were young, but as she had matured so had his feelings for her. When he awoke every morning, he felt the pull to be in her presence. No day was satisfactory that did not include her. As for Olivia, she evidently enjoyed his company, but as a brother more than a lover.

Their regular debates invigorated him, their discussions on philosophy engaged his faculties, and her sense of wonder at all things scientific delighted him. By comparison, other women were vacuous and shallow. He had no interest in marriage to such a woman.

"I must go to Jackson. He has news of some fencing that needs repair. I shall see you at dinnertime." He made for the door.

"Dinner? Not tea?" His mother's weary eyes widened with disappointment.

"I am taking tea with the Deverells, if you recall."

The dowager's lips flattened. "You spend altogether too much time with that family." She folded her handkerchief into a square. "I feel the lack of you so greatly."

He was torn.

He felt the filial duty to entertain his mother deeply, but her company was stifling. She had no interest in the butterflies he collected from around the estate, no

11

inclination to review the world stage and positively no disposition for debate. These were found in plentiful supply at Worcester Park. The Deverells had done little to confine their young daughters' natural curiosity about the world. Instead, the girls were given great encouragement in satisfying their intellect and broadening their minds. Though they encouraged the now grown girls to steer their interests into accepted cultural pursuits, Olivia would not comply. He often imagined her at Oxford, chuckling at the idea that she would outshine all the male undergraduates.

The Deverell girls' progressive education had spoiled him. He craved their company above all others. The thought that he would be forced to marry a woman whose thoughts went no further than the menu for dinner or the state of the silverware, was depressing.

He strode back from the door and took her hands in his. "It is the first time this week that I have left you for tea, Mother. And I will be full of their news to share with you at dinner this evening. That is something to look forward to, is it not?"

Her lips remained in a firm line, but she lifted soulful eyes to him. "I suppose it will have to do."

The muffled laughter on the other side of the drawing room door beckoned Jeremy and a smile tugged at his lips. From the banging and knocking, he imagined they were playing with their dog, an energetic spaniel by the name of Hercules.

As the maid opened the door, a flash of blue and a dainty shoe confirmed his suspicions.

"Oh, hello Jeremy," said Felicity from the floor, the youngest of the sisters. "Hercules has stolen my other shoe."

He was as comfortable at Worcester Park as he was in his own home, perhaps more. The sisters had provided companionship for him in his youth, indeed he considered them more as sisters than friends. How his feelings for Olivia had transitioned it was hard to tell.

"Jeremy!" exclaimed Olivia, pulling him into a platonic embrace. "I am eager to share with you my morning's discoveries." She lowered her voice as she dropped his hands. "I have some questions concerning Descartes that I must discuss with you."

She pulled him into a little alcove and nodded at Genevieve to bring him some tea while the rest of the room continued to watch Felicity chase the dog.

Reaching for his hand again, he could hardly concentrate on her words as her touch ignited such a spark in him.

"I have read this very morning that Descartes believes we are all endowed with innate knowledge from God. What do you say? Are we re-discovering things we already know or is every new fact a revelation?"

"Good day to you too." He laughed as her serious eyes engaged his. "Can a man finish his tea before being grilled about philosophy?"

Honey curls framed her oval face, escaping the braids that crossed her head. "Of course," she said with her classic good nature. "I get so excited I forget to let people settle in sometimes."

"Indeed, you do," declared Jeremy, taking a sip from his cup as the dog streaked by with the shoe clasped between his white teeth. Felicity followed close behind.

"Entertain us with a merry tune, Julia," said Mrs. Deverell over the chaos.

Julia happily strode over to the beautiful instrument and lifting the lid began to play a boisterous melody, without the need of any sheet music.

"How propitious!" declared Olivia. "The music will allow us to speak and not betray to Mother that I am discussing a subject she does not entirely approve of." Her light blue eyes sparkled with excitement. "I have been

13

subjected to fittings and proddings and pokes for a good part of the morning."

"I wonder you had any time for Descartes," replied Jeremy.

"I sneaked into the library before Mother could find me this morning. How have I never discovered Descartes before now?" Her brows rose in arcs that lifted her features into such an expression that he had to hold onto his hand so as not to reach up and place it on her soft cheek.

Instead, he laughed. "As progressive as your parents are, even they have their limits. I do not believe Descartes is considered approved curriculum for today's gentlewomen, Olivia. You are in a class of your own to find such interest in the fellow."

For the next twenty minutes they bantered back and forth as Jeremy reached into the recesses of his mind to recall his tutor's lessons on the French philosopher.

"When do you leave for London?" he asked, her questions exhausted.

"In a fortnight. You know I would much rather stay here but Mother and Father insist."

"Would it make the arrangement less daunting if I were to tell you that I will be in town too?" he asked. He had resisted telling her until now because he had not truly resolved to go until this very moment. He could not bear the thought of her regaled in new feminine fashions and not be a witness to it—as much as it might pain him to see her courted by other men.

Olivia threw up her hands. "Oh, Jeremy! I should be much less intimidated by everything if I know that you are there." Her head tilted to the side. "Why are you going?"

The truth would hardly be appropriate.

"Mother wishes me to go. She says it is high time I found myself a wife."

He watched her carefully. The light, that had moments before lit her vibrant eyes, dimmed, and his heart caught.

14

"A wife?" Her brow knitted and her lips pursed in such a pretty pout that he could hardly refrain from staring at them. "Why do we have to grow up?" she continued. "Why can we not stay as children with no responsibilities? If you have a wife, she will surely not welcome my presence all the time."

Julia had changed to playing a mournful tune that fit his current feelings.

"Then I shall be forced to make your company part of the marriage negotiations," he said with a small smile. "And what of your husband? Will he welcome me?"

"I shall refuse any man that cannot accept our friendship," she declared, a hint of pink showing on her cheek. "Which reminds me. Do you know of a Stephen Manwaring?"

His heart dropped. He knew well of the man whose star was rising in the scientific world. So, *he* had caught Olivia's attention.

"The scientist? I have heard him speak once or twice."

"What is he like?" she asked, her spine crouching over with interest.

He could lie, but it was beneath him. "He is a fine fellow and an engaging speaker."

She bit her cheek. "Is he very old?"

Jeremy could not stop a guffaw of laughter escaping his lips. "Old? If two and thirty be considered old then, yes."

"Julia was teasing me that he might be as old as Father." The frown upon her face was enchanting.

"No, no." He thought of the man he had heard in London the summer before, a tall, solid man with a heavy brow and prominent features. "For an academic admitted into the ranks of the Royal Society, I believe he is considered quite young."

"I have heard that he will be in London while I am there. Do you think you could arrange a meeting?" Her

15

expression was that of a child who fears her request for a second crumpet will be denied.

"Though I cannot admit to being an acquaintance, I will do what I can."

Though he dearly wanted to refuse, he could not. He never had been able to ignore her requests. Such was her power over him.

Chapter 3

Olivia

S tanding on the pavement, Olivia looked up at her aunt's fashionable townhome from under her umbrella. Its white Grecian pillars and black iron railings glistened in the downpour. Above the door was a small balcony off the main receiving room. Large symmetrical windows on either side streamed with raindrops and bright flowers in window boxes trembled under the weight of the moisture.

The fancy reticule on her wrist was bumping against her forearm and the new, dainty shoes were taking in water. She hoisted her skirts and started up the slippery steps. Her shrinking-violet of a cousin, Mary, hovered near the door, eyes darting suspiciously to the rain as if it might melt her if she stepped out.

As they pushed into the grand foyer, servants took their umbrellas and outerwear, flicking the rain onto the tile which would be mopped immediately.

"How lovely to see you," murmured Mary, her voice frail as old lace though she had not seen her twenty-third birthday. "Do follow me."

Removing her bonnet and shaking her hair, Olivia walked across the black and white marble and up the stairs to the drawing room, where sat her Aunt Frances in a chair that was reminiscent of a throne. Her aunt's round head had long since swallowed her neck and she was so large in girth that walking was only accomplished with severe difficulty.

Lady Frances Roquefort was her mother's oldest sister. She had married a third son, whose two older brothers had died, leaving him the title of earl, and now, as the only titled member of her family, lauded over everyone. Olivia had tried to like her aunt, but her condescension was wearing. And she took a dim view of the liberal education of her nieces. Fortunately, their interactions with the family were few and far between but since the Deverell's did not own a London townhouse, they were obligated to stay with the Roqueforts for Olivia's season.

"Georgina," she said addressing Olivia's mother. "I should have told you that long sleeves are no longer in." Her mother's false smile slipped. "And Olivia, come, let me look at you." Olivia stepped forward for inspection feeling like a prize pig at a county fair. Her aunt held up spectacles on a stick like opera glasses. Her large chin tilted up as she looked down her considerable nose.

"Yes," she finally admitted. "You are greatly improved." It was a compliment delivered like an accusation for none of her own daughters were beauties.

Olivia's father, Charles Deverell, bowed over his sister-in-law's sausage-like fingers and then they all sat upon silk chaises that were rather uncomfortable with no support for one's back. Wan Mary occupied a plush chair next to her mother.

"So, we are here to find you a husband," Frances said slowly as though considering the thought as she spoke.

Her delivery made Olivia shudder. Why did her aunt have to make the endeavor sound so mercenary?

Noticing that her daughter was not going to respond, Georgina Deverell filled the silence. "Sister, we are so grateful for your hospitality, aren't we Charles? There are so few opportunities for meeting new people deep in our part of the countryside."

Aunt Frances shuddered. "And it is so damp in Worcestershire!"

Olivia felt the hackles rise at the criticism of her beloved Worcester but pushed them down, biting her tongue. Now was definitely *not* the occasion for a debate.

"I hope you are ready to engage," continued her aunt. "For there is a ball at Lady Cunningham's this very evening."

Olivia was participating in the formalities under a certain degree of duress. She loved a ball, but among her own friends where she could relax. Here, in London, she would be among strangers and the rules of etiquette would be far more strict. She had hoped for a small reprieve after their long journey and was thus more than a little disappointed.

"Whatever you think best, sister," replied Olivia's mother with a slight worry line above her fine brows.

"I trust Olivia has new gowns for her season?"

Mrs. Deverell crossed her hands on her lap. "Of course!"

"Good!" declared her aunt with narrowed eyes. "Let us hope they are not *too* out of fashion. Now, let me call the servants to take you up to your rooms."

In less than five minutes, they had been dismissed.

Lady Cunningham's London home was best described as a small palace. It was not in a row of houses but set in a small park. The façade was lit with torches that gave the red bricks a welcoming glow, and the Deverells now sat in a line of coaches with their fine relatives, waiting to descend.

Cousin Mary was wearing a very modern dress and feathered hat that outshone her looks by several degrees. An expression of condescension had settled on her face ever since Olivia had descended the stairs and it was obvious that the new gown was not quite of the latest London style. For her part, Olivia did not care about such things as the current fashions, and she was so unaffected by what her dowdy cousin Mary thought that she had to bite back a smile at the ridiculous headpiece.

She peered out of the window, witnessing countless hopeful young women alighting from carriages and mounting the stone steps. How would she stand out among such a crowd?

The carriage pulled to a stop, and they exited. The air was chilly but did not warrant a cape. Their journey up the front steps was slowed by the ample Aunt Frances who had to be helped up by both her husband and daughter, causing a bottleneck of guests behind them.

The crowd moved as a wave and Olivia had little time to examine the general splendor of the foyer as she was carried into the massive ballroom that was lighted by a thousand candles that revealed a delightful fresco on the high ceiling. The atmosphere was festive, and she caught her breath, surprised by her own excitement.

Once Aunt Frances was settled in a chair that provided the best view of the dancers, for she would not move from the spot all night, Olivia was bombarded by young men seeking to fill up her dance card. She suppressed a giggle. She was unused to such male attentions and it made her giddy.

When the current dance was at an end, the first young man who had signed her card, a gangly youth, strode toward her, dressed in bright military uniform, brass epaulettes shining. She checked with her mother who nodded approval and allowed him to escort her to the floor.

"Second Lieutenant John McEnnany at your service," he declared, bowing deeply before taking her hand for the quadrille.

"Olivia Deverell of Worcester," she replied, allowing him to set their place in the square.

The orchestra began and Lieutenant McEnnany moved with an enthusiasm that outshone the ability of his feet to keep up. The dance was fast, leaving little time for chatter but as they waited for another couple to gallop down the line he asked her, "Worcester? I can't say I know the county."

"It is one of England's finest, though I dare say I am a little biased," she replied.

The speed of the dance caused their conversation to be stilted but when he asked about her pastimes she told him of her penchant for philosophy. "Are you an enthusiast?" she asked.

The smile on his face dropped a little. "Philosophy? Only if it is the philosophy of warfare," he replied with a crooked grin. "That is an unusual interest for a lady, if you don't mind me saying so," he continued.

She ducked under their linked arms. "Not at all. I am rather proud of the fact that I am an *unusual* woman."

"Ah." The cadence of the syllable was such that she doubted he would be searching her out at any other balls.

The second dance was with a portly young man, whose buttons were fighting desperately to keep his stomach covered. He was surprisingly light on his feet, but the glistening of his upper lip betrayed the cost. His conversation was minimal as he concentrated all his efforts into the dance.

By the third set, she was feeling the need of a respite. Her energetic partner chattered endlessly and was uninterested in hearing from her at all, it seemed. As he escorted her back to her seat, she felt flushed with exertion. The air in the room was thick with rosewater and pomade and her head was swimming with the music of the waltz. Additionally, her ankle was beginning to ache. She yearned for fresh air and repose.

She glanced at her card. Algernon Longbottom. With a name like that he deserved to be abandoned. Her mother was busy in conversation and her father was nowhere to be seen—probably smoking cigars in a library somewhere. Good.

Shouldering her way through the gaggle of debutantes lining the walls, she made for the French windows. The pins in her hair were beginning to itch and she wanted nothing more than to tear down the whole house of curls.

She lunged for the s-shaped filigree handle and pushed down, releasing the life-giving air from outside that washed over her like a wave at the seaside. She slid through, closing the door behind her and limped across the gravel to a stone bench. Sinking onto the seat she ripped off her slipper and rubbed the offending ankle.

"Not to your tastes in there?"

Her hand slammed to her chest as she peered into the dark where the familiar voice had originated.

"Jeremy!" she cried. "You scared me half to death."

He peeled himself from the shadows and came to sit beside her, legs astride, necktie loosened.

"Too much dancing?" he asked nodding to her ankle.

"Altogether too much," she replied.

"Let me massage it," he said, starting to slide down to the gravel.

"No!" she declared. "Not here!" Even she knew that to be found outside alone, in London, with a young man who was holding her ankle would raise eyebrows and tarnish her reputation.

His brows pinched together. "Whyever not? I do it all the time at Worcester Park, do I not?"

"This is different," she warned. "Among strangers it would cause a scandal."

Jeremy chuckled and the familiarity of it warmed her. "It is not immoral, Olivia."

"I know that, but we cannot control other people's conclusions. I suspect that the wagging tongues are eager to pounce on any perceived impropriety. You are like my brother, but no one here would understand." Her tone turned playful. "Besides it is my first night here in London. I don't want to blot my copy book already."

He took a sip from the glass in his hand. "Since when did you care what others think of you?"

"Since Mama and Papa have gone to so much effort to ensure I have a season."

"Even though you didn't really want one?"

She cut her eyes over to him. "It is true that I had little say in the matter, but I *will* make an effort for Mama and Papa. This means so much to them." She kicked the ground. "But I am sure you know that I would rather not be paraded about town like a filly to be sold." The words had spilled out unchecked.

"I know only too well." He reached out for her hand, but she whipped it away. "What have I done to deserve that?" he asked.

"Nothing, but I must guard my reputation, Jeremy. I am already compromised by being outside alone with you. The rules are different here." She slipped her foot back into the white dancing slipper.

"I am surprised that you have become so conventional so soon," he said.

"Do not tease me. I owe it to my family to be on my best behavior—at least until after I am presented at the Queen Charlotte Ball. I may not embrace all that is London society but I will not intentionally dent my family's reputation in the eyes of the Court." She grinned. "However hard it may be."

He leaned back against the wall of the house. "How are you enjoying your first ball?"

She did not temper her impression. "All the men I have met so far seem to be boobies. Present company excepted."

"Well, I am glad to know that you value my intelligence." He lifted his glass as if he were joining a toast.

Olivia glared at his obtuse manner. "Not one of the men I have danced with could hold an intelligent conversation. How can I be expected to marry anyone as silly as that?"

23

"Then marry me."

Olivia slapped his arm. "Do be serious, Jeremy."

"Careful, someone may think you are trying to hold my hand and start a rumor."

She rolled her eyes. "I suppose I deserved that." Running a hand across her neck she continued. "But it seems I am expected to marry someone to settle my future and allow my sisters their turn, so I will continue on with this charade."

They both stopped talking and stared out into the dark garden. The wispy clouds parted revealing a crescent moon and the constellations around it.

A giggle started to push its way through her corset until it bubbled out of her mouth of its own volition.

"What is so funny?" asked Jeremy, his voice deeper than usual.

"Algernon Longbottom. That was the name of my next dance partner," she explained. "What hope does a man have with a name like that?"

"How shallow you are," Jeremy complained, dragging his sole through the gravel. "How do you know that he is not the most intelligent man at the ball tonight? If we men are to be judged by our names alone what chance do any of us have?"

"I suppose it is very naughty of me." She turned on the bench to face him. "How are *you* enjoying yourself?"

He shrugged his shoulders. "I face the same problem as you. I have danced with seven girls, who have not an ounce of intelligence between them."

Olivia twisted her mouth. "I thought the requirements for a good wife were simply to be a pretty appendage on the arm and to produce an heir."

"That may be the case for the vast majority of gentleman but alas, I demand more than that," he replied, getting to his feet. "Your family has spoiled me. All you Deverell girls are capable of intelligent conversation. It means that I cannot tolerate a woman who is an empty shell."

"Even Felicity?"

"She may not have reached the heights of education that you and your other sisters have, but she is a great deal more clever than any of the girls in that room." He nodded toward the ballroom.

"Your wife is somewhere out there," declared Olivia.

Jeremy mumbled something she could not discern.

"What did you say?"

"I merely said, I hope so."

Olivia did not think that is what he had really said but let the matter rest.

The music began to fade.

"I must go back before I am missed," she said, turning to Jeremy whose eyes were glinting in the moonlight. "I wish I could dance with you, but my card is full."

"What a waste that would be since we dance all the time at Worcester Park."

"You are right," she agreed, moving her shoulders to reposition her short corset as though she were gearing up for battle.

She stepped toward the window and felt a tugging. She looked behind to see Jeremy holding the ribbon that ran around her dress. She tipped her head as a smile curled her lips.

"You should know you look beautiful," he said, his cobalt eyes more serious than she could ever remember.

She dropped her lashes to her cheek. "Why thank you, but I shall never be as pretty as Genevieve."

Jeremy snorted. "There is more to beauty than a pretty face, Olivia. Much more. You should never feel inferior to any of your sisters."

She pulled the ribbon and he let it slide through his lithe fingers. Then grasping the latch, she opened the glass door and the music spilled into the garden.

In two steps, Jeremy was at her side, taking her in his arms and twirling her around the patio. She allowed her head to hang back and surrendered to the rhythm. Why could not all men be like Jeremy?

When the music completely stopped, she curtsied and ran to the door, but glancing back, she was confused to see sadness painted on his dear, familiar face.

What could be ailing him?

Chapter 4
Jeremy

As Jeremy watched Olivia walk through the glass door, his heart beat a tattoo in his chest. The silky feel of her ribbon lingered on his fingers. A desire to kiss her had almost consumed him as they waltzed around the patio.

Perhaps coming to London had been a bad idea.

He remained by the glass, observing as she walked back to her party, the ringlets in her hair swaying with each step. It was a pleasurable torture. He sighed deeply as a young man of medium build with enviable whiskers came to claim her for the next set.

She smiled up at him and allowed herself to be led to the floor. Jeremy scowled as he leaned a jealous shoulder against the window frame, powerless to take his eyes from her.

He stayed until content that she had nothing but contempt for the man and decided to find distraction in a game of cards or some such in the library.

The deep rumble of males in conversation could be heard above the music in the background and he pushed into a room filled with men, seated around a masculine, smoke filled study.

At the center was a man he recognized—Stephen Manwaring. He was in full lecture mode and Jeremy slipped in, taking occupancy of a leather club chair that was vacant in the back of the room.

The scientist was in the middle of recounting his last voyage to a secluded island in the South Pacific where he had studied several unique forms of wildlife.

Jeremy examined him with new eyes as he spoke, knowing of Olivia's desire to meet him. Manwaring was in his early thirties, but time exposed on the deck of ships had weathered his skin which was tanned and bore evidence of premature lines. But he spoke with passion and was an engaging storyteller, his audience hanging on every word. Jeremy paid little attention to the content of his speech, instead pondering his stance, his gait, and the shape of his head. His dark eyes were alive, content to be the center of attention, and his jaw was sharp as though he had missed a meal or two. Would he be attractive to Olivia? Jeremy could not tell.

Rather than exposing the bare facts of his travels, Manwaring was skilled at weaving in a sense of adventure and danger. No wonder the man had already made his mark on the scientific world.

Another fifteen minutes passed and Manwaring ended his recitation with a theatrical flourish of his arms. The room broke into spontaneous applause.

Manwaring's smug smile betrayed his love of the admiration.

As he vacated the center of the room, men of all ages crowded round him, full of questions. Jeremy stood, waiting his turn, watching Manwaring handle their questions with ease and confidence.

"How can I help you?" His question to Jeremy was sincere and he felt himself come under the spell of the man.

"We have met before," said Jeremy by way of introduction. "You spoke at the townhall in Chiswick after Christmas. You were debating the morality of cadaver dissection."

"And did you agree with my conclusion?" Mr. Manwaring asked with good humor.

"I did, in fact," Jeremy responded.

"Then you must be a fine chap," he replied, slapping Jeremy's shoulder. "And what do you do?"

"I am an earl," replied Jeremy. "I oversee a large estate in Worcestershire."

The smile dropped from the scientist's friendly face. "Oh, should I refer to you as my Lord?"

Jeremy waved the notion away. "Please don't. You can call me Jeremy. Jeremy Worthington."

The wilted smile rekindled. "Then I am happy to meet you, Jeremy."

Jeremy tilted his head and spoke before the impulse passed. "I have a friend who is anxious to meet you."

"Bring him here! I am not an enthusiast or a proficient at dancing to tell the truth and am only here at the request of my sister, Vivienne. I shall be happy for an excuse to stay away from the ladies."

Jeremy laughed at the irony. "It is not a 'he' but a 'she' who desires to meet you."

"Indeed." Manwaring grasped his hands together, a gold ring on his little finger winking in the light. "I am intrigued."

"She is a childhood friend and the most intelligent woman of my acquaintance. She knows of you and is eager for an introduction."

"When you say 'intelligent' I suppose that you mean she is proficient in the French language and plays the piano," he responded, with a slight wink.

Manwaring's prejudice grated. "Olivia Deverell cares little for French and is hopeless at the piano. No, when I say she is intelligent I mean that she is learned in the sciences and reads Descartes for pleasure."

Manwaring's brows rose, and he sucked in his hollow cheeks. "A revolutionary then? A bluestocking!"

Jeremy chuckled at the idea of Olivia being cast as a revolutionary. "In many ways yes, though do not expect her to arrive at a ball in breeches. She is traditional enough in her dress and has enough beauty to satisfy any man."

Manwaring's thick brows rose. "Your description has intrigued me, Jeremy. I should very much like to meet this exceptional woman."

Though a ball of dread was growing in his middle, Jeremy said, "I can take you to her immediately, but I would recommend not telling her who you are. Her eagerness will translate into a tying of the tongue, I don't doubt, which will give you a false impression. Let us play a little trick on her so that she remains at ease, and I wager less than a minute into the dance she will demand a debate on some topic or other."

"Though I hate to dance, I accept the challenge," Manwaring declared with enthusiasm. "Let me introduce myself." He bowed low. "Joshua Thorn at your service."

Jeremy's eyes crinkled as he ignored his misgivings. "A very suitable name for an ordinary gentleman," he agreed. "Come! Let us test your wits against hers."

Chapter 5

Olivia

The ballroom seemed even more stuffy when she returned from outside than it had earlier, as Olivia checked her card. One more name and then she had a break. She looked longingly toward the patio and could see Jeremy looking doleful.

Her next partner was a tall, thin man with little to say for himself who completely clammed up after a probing question. As the set was ending, her ankle began throbbing again and all she could think of was escape. She turned in the direction of the French windows, exerting great effort not to limp. However, just as a sly departure for the patio was within reach, she heard her name.

Jeremy.

She turned to see him with another gentleman and swallowed the words she was going to say. The older stranger was angular with a heavy brow, prominent cheek bones, and a smile that softened his rugged features. She pulled a smile from somewhere and met his gaze.

"Olivia, I must introduce you to my friend Joshua Thorn. No partner for this one? I propose that you two dance this one together."

She cast a frown at Jeremy, but his features were fixed like a statue.

She knew the next dance to be a Viennese waltz which was demanding of both body and breath, but Jeremy had placed her in this awkward position where to refuse would have been bad mannered.

She would have words with him later.

Olivia lifted her arm, and the older man took her hand and placed a kiss upon it.

"I would be honored," he said, his tone smooth and deep. He led her to the floor to join the swift current of couples already spinning on their toes.

"Where are you from?" he asked as they slipped into the tide, his feet taking a moment to find the rhythm.

"Worcester. Do you know it?" Speech at such a rate was going to be a challenge.

He looked up from his feet. "I do not. I am from Northampton myself."

It took all her effort not to wince as her ankle took the full force of the pirouette type steps. "I have never been to Northampton. How do you like it?"

"It is an average place with average people," he replied.

His conversation was not inspiring and the pain in her foot was becoming an emergency. It was time to test his mettle.

She bit her lip. "How do you know Jeremy?"

"We met at…a meeting. Rather tedious stuff, I'm afraid." Now that he was settled in the flow, he maneuvered her quite well.

Her mouth pinched into a determined line. "What are your feelings on the subject of innate knowledge from God?"

Joshua Thorn reared back his head as he turned her and let out a roaring laugh. It was not unpleasant but had a sharp tone to it.

"What serious talk for a ball," he said, his dark, inquisitive eyes peering into hers. "I thought subjects were restricted to the amount of people, the quality of the music, and the fine dresses."

Her ankle was getting weaker and weaker by the moment as the demanding dance continued endlessly, on and on. It was time to be rid of this insipid man. "Life is too short for such mundane chatter, don't you agree?"

To her surprise his expression transformed. "As a matter of fact, I do."

His response was so unexpected that for a moment she was at a loss for words. Recovering, she asked, "Well?"

Another couple bumped into them, and a sharp pain ran down her foot. It was just the excuse she needed. "Ouch!" She crumpled into Mr. Thorn's arms.

"Good heavens, Miss Deverell! Are you hurt?" he asked.

"I think I twisted my ankle," she lied, relishing the sweet relief of pressure from her foot.

He put his arm under hers, lifting her weight, and gently led her from the floor to her seat. She sank down, thankful for the respite, the offending appendage throbbing with pain from the energetic dance.

"May I get you something?" he asked. The concern on his face appeared to be genuine and her heart softened toward him slightly.

"No, no. Rest is all I need. It will be fine." She hoped this public 'accident' would allow her to sit for the rest of the evening.

Mrs. Deverell approached, worried eyes darting between Olivia and her partner. Olivia knew her mother was choosing her words carefully.

"Is everything alright?" The sharp line drawn between her eyes betrayed her concern.

"An errant couple bumped us and caused Miss Deverell to twist her ankle," explained Mr. Thorn before she could answer for herself.

Her mother's eyes shot to Olivia's and a silent signal passed between them. "Thank you for helping her from the floor Mr…?"

"Manwaring," he said, taking Mrs. Deverell's hand. "Stephen Manwaring."

A sharp knife plunged into Olivia's breast. *Manwaring?* Her eyes flashed to the man who had introduced himself as Joshua Thorn.

Head hanging to his chest and eyes hooded, he looked abashed. "I am sorry for the subterfuge, Miss Deverell. Jeremy Worthington and I had a little wager. He assured me that you were quite a species apart from your sex and bet that you would engage me in a philosophical debate before the end of one dance." He bowed. "He was correct. It was utterly refreshing."

Olivia's mind scattered like a scared rabbit, and she wished the ground to open up and swallow her. This man was not a tiresome nobody, but the eminent scientist and man of learning she had hoped to meet.

She grabbed the skin of her neck. "I...should never...have..." she stammered.

"It is quite alright," he assured her. "This is the very reason I used a pseudonym. Mr. Worthington thought you might not be able to act yourself if you knew who I was. I am very glad that you did. Now, if I can no longer be of assistance, I shall leave you to recover." He smiled down at her. "Perhaps we can meet again when you are feeling better?"

He bowed low and walked away as Olivia gawked, mouth agape.

Her mother plonked into the seat beside her. "Should I know him?"

Olivia expelled a hot breath of shame. "He is only the most famous young scientist of our time." She gripped the fabric of her skirts. "Oh! What a fool I have made of myself!"

Her mother spread out her fan. "Really? Do you seek to curry favor with that gentleman?"

"Mother, I had great hopes of meeting him during my season. He is exactly the kind of person I should like to make the acquaintance of." She dragged a finger across her cheek. "I knew that Mr. Manwaring was on a lecture tour here and hoped to attend one. Now I have ruined it all. He will consider me a silly woman and will never like me now." Tears of humiliation stung her eyes like a thousand needles.

"There, there." Her mother patted her arm. "One thing you are not is silly. Did he not just say he wishes to see you again?"

Olivia started. "Did he?" She tried to recall his last words but her mind was too agitated by heightened emotions that fought like alley cats in her chest.

"He certainly did," replied her mother, fanning herself. "*And* he knows your name. I shall expect an invitation forthwith." She turned in her seat and lowered her voice. "Now, what shall we do about that ankle. I'm sure I don't know why it gives you such grief. It must be a defect from birth."

Chapter 6
Jeremy

The breakfast room at Jeremy's home in Cadogan Square was his favorite. It caught the morning sun and brightened many a stormy mood. His mother had remodeled it when she was a young bride and instead of heavy oaks, she had chosen to paint the wainscoting a pleasing cream and line the walls with floral, dainty wallpaper. The large, bowed windows were hung with delicate, sheer, lace curtains while the sides were festooned with a cheerful chintz. It was joyful and inviting.

His dark temper this morning, however, could not be improved. He had watched Olivia and Stephen Manwaring from across the room last night with acute interest. He knew that she had asked him a probing question when he saw the man throw back his head and a twist of envy had opened in his stomach. Then she had crumpled into Manwaring's arms, and it had taken all his willpower not to run to her assistance. He knew the demanding dance would put a strain on her ankle.

The instant Manwaring had revealed his true identity, a ghost of humiliation had passed over her features and he felt the stirrings of guilt. She would be very angry with him for tricking her, but it was for her own good. Jeremy knew that she would be too nervous if she was aware of who Manwaring was from the beginning and had felt a righteous pride knowing that he was laying his own desires on the altar for her good. He tried to push the remorse away, but it had taken up residence.

A couple of days for her to cool off might be in order.

Now, as he flicked through his mail, he was left to ponder the fact that it was most inconvenient that Stephen

Manwaring was a personable fellow. On some level, Jeremy had always believed that if he waited long enough Olivia would see him as a viable option for a husband, but now that Manwaring had entered the field, doubts were springing up like unwanted weeds in a flower garden.

Checking the paper, he saw that his opponent was scheduled to speak at the British Museum that afternoon and planned to attend.

Keep your enemies close.

The British Museum, housed in Montagu House in Bloomsbury, gleamed in the afternoon sun, its façade of seventeen bay windows making it one of London's grandest old houses. Built for the First Duke of Montagu it was sold to the trustees of the British Museum in 1759. It was the first museum of its kind in the world and often hosted lectures by the great minds of the day.

A few other late stragglers were climbing the steps as the hour chimed and Jeremy hurried to follow them.

The lecture room was smaller than he had expected with seats for about fifty people. As he slunk in, Stephen Manwaring tipped his head in acknowledgement. So much for remaining in the shadows.

A gentleman with enormous, curly, gray whiskers was introducing Manwaring and listing his many accomplishments. Manwaring was trying to appear modest but was failing to conceal a pretentious smirk of satisfaction.

The man who came to stand at the podium this afternoon was much more serious than the person he had met at the ball. His sharp jaw was firm and his eye steady as he began his exposition on the flora and fauna he had studied on his latest voyage.

Though less entertaining than the tale he had spun at the ball, Jeremy could not help but admire the man's knowledge and expertise. He looked around the room. Most of the men appeared to be in their late fifties with a sprinkling of men in their thirties and only himself and one other appearing younger. No women, of course.

The mouth of envy in his stomach gaped wider.

Stephen Manwaring was exactly the kind of man who might attract Olivia. Though he was not handsome in the traditional sense, he carried a poise that stemmed from confidence, and his intelligence rendered his eyes worthy of consideration.

By comparison, Jeremy considered himself more handsome than Manwaring though he certainly wasn't the most good-looking man around town. However, he could not claim such depth of knowledge or fame as the man currently giving the lecture.

When the discourse was over and the question portion finished, the men in the room applauded. Some left but others crowded around him like proverbial bees around the honeypot. Jeremy hung back, watching as the man bathed in the glow of his glory.

When the last man was preparing to leave, Jeremy stepped forward.

"Very interesting," he began, "though I don't know how you stand to be on a ship for so long. I am a lover of creature comforts myself."

Manwaring's face furrowed with sympathy and understanding. "I don't mind admitting to you that the lack of water and the quality of the company is wearing at times but my excitement for the subject matter overcomes all those inconveniences." He collected his notes and placed them in a leather satchel. "Are you interested in science?"

"I admit to more than a passing interest, though I have no desire to go on an exploration such as you do—much prefer to read about your findings in the newspaper by a roaring fire," Jeremy chuckled.

"Shame! We could do with a young, vigorous man such as yourself." He stacked some books on the lectern and slung the satchel over his shoulder. "Why don't you join me at my club?"

The Socrates Club in Covent Garden was a small dark establishment close enough to the market to hear the hue and cry of the sellers. An elderly, butler-type guarded the desk but upon seeing Stephen, his wrinkled face split into a genuine smile.

"Mr. Manwaring. It is wonderful to see you again. I see you have brought a guest. Will you both be staying for dinner?"

"Pearson, good to see you." Manwaring cast a questioning expression at Jeremy who nodded. "Yes, thank you."

Manwaring led Jeremy to a room in which a debate was in full swing. Rich, carved paneling covered the walls along with several oil paintings. Leather chairs surrounded small tables with the occasional buttoned sofa. The ceiling was smooth plaster adorned with grapes and garlands. A large bay window stretching from the ceiling to the floor allowed the afternoon sun to penetrate, and light sconces punctuated the walls at intervals.

The air was thick with smoke and Jeremy suppressed a cough.

"I put it to you that the mathematical order of the natural world is evidence of the existence of God," cried one man who was waving his arms to emphasize his point.

"How do you account for chaos, then?" cried another man, holding a tumbler of whiskey.

"Purely man's interference," responded the first.

"What say you?" said the drinker, indicating Manwaring with his tumbler so that some of the amber liquid spilled out. All the men in the room turned.

"I am with your opponent," declared Manwaring. "My explorations lead me to believe that an ordered intelligence is behind all creation."

Jeremy settled himself into a chair and watched with interest as the debate billowed around him. Back and forth the speakers went, each with his own opinion, little ready to be swayed by another's argument.

At length the debate lost steam without a resolution and Manwaring came to sit by Jeremy, his cheeks bright from the debate.

"Is it like this all the time?" asked Jeremy.

"On any given day one can join any number of debates ranging from the existence of other planets to the need for cleanliness in the slums."

"I should find it exhausting," Jeremy admitted. "The Deverell sisters enjoy a good debate and that is about all I can stand."

Manwaring removed his jacket and loosened the knot at his neck. "On the contrary, I find the whole thing invigorating! Tell me more about these Deverells."

"You have met Olivia—"

"Yes, do you know she asked me my stand on innate knowledge? At a ball! Thoroughly original."

"Olivia is an enigma to be sure. Even among her sisters she is the most interested in learning. Her passions run to science, history, and philosophy. Though her family has always encouraged their four girls to satisfy their appetites in regard to knowledge, Olivia has taken it to such an extreme that even *her* progressive parents are beginning to disapprove. They fear that so much education will elevate her above her male counterparts, that she will unwittingly make herself unattractive to the opposite sex. Men are such proud creatures, are we not? And her parents understand only too well the need to find husbands for their daughters."

40

A smile tugged at Manwaring's lips. "Though I have no interest in matrimony at present, Olivia Deverell is exactly the kind of person that might change my mind."

Jealousy swirled but Jeremy knew this was what Olivia desired. Or thought she did.

"What is your interest in the girl?" Manwaring asked Jeremy.

It would be so easy to thwart any opposition right now, but unless Olivia had experience of what the world had to offer, she would not be content. The risk of course, was that he would lose her forever. His stomach churned as he said, "They are my neighbors. I have known them all my life." He took a deep breath and plunged in before he lost his courage. "You should come to a dinner at my house. I will arrange for you to sit by Olivia, and you can debate to your heart's content."

"I should like that very much," he said crossing his legs. "And what of the sisters?"

"Olivia is the most progressive. The next sister, Julia, is a talented natural musician who makes any piano sing under her fingers. She is followed by Genevieve, a true beauty who is constantly championing the needs of the poor and illiterate. She believes that all members of society should be able to read and write."

"In that I agree with her," declared Manwaring. "I am of the opinion that education will lift the lower classes from their poverty which will benefit society as a whole."

"Then there is little Felicity who at fourteen is still under construction," continued Jeremy. "She is showing great potential as an artist. And growing up with such sisters, she is bound to follow their lead in forward thinking."

"What a lively household!" the scientist declared.

"You have no idea!" agreed Jeremy.

A waiter came to get their drink order, and after he retired Manwaring said, "I hope that Miss Deverell's ankle is improved. She twisted it while we danced."

41

Olivia was extremely sensitive about her limp. She took great pains to conceal it. A war of loyalties battled within Jeremy. Again presented with the opportunity to subvert any opposition to her affections, at great personal cost, he chose the path less traveled and put her desires before his own.

He adjusted his shirt cuffs before replying. "I could not tell you. I have not seen her today."

A servant in full Livery announced dinner.

Manwaring stood. "Shall we?"

Chapter 7

Olivia

The townhome in Cadogan Square was new to Olivia. She had known Jeremy all her life but had never once been here. It differed from her aunt's in that the entire exterior was bowed and a spectacular, black iron grating ran across the front under the windows of the first floor.

She was still angry that Jeremy had deceived her the night of the ball and at the first opportunity she would give him a piece of her mind. The invitation to dine had included her aunt's family too and since it had arrived on the embossed stationary of *The Earl of Barclay*, Aunt Frances was suitably impressed.

Olivia would skewer him here in a private moment.

As she allowed the servants to take her cape, her thoughts went to her ankle. She had spent the previous day resting and could only feel the slightest twinge now. She would sit out the Viennese waltz in future.

They were conducted to a drawing room where Jeremy met them. She had to hold back a giggle. Seeing him greet her aunt and cousin was like watching a play. His manner in his role as the earl was so formal and his conversation so proper. She had never seen him like this, though he had held the title since he was fifteen, and it felt awkward and unreal.

She looked around the room with its cheerful curtains and light walls—clearly the interior had been designed by a woman.

"How are you this evening, Olivia?"

She narrowed her eyes at him. "There is no need to put on airs with me," she chided. Something about him seemed different, perhaps he had styled his hair differently or was it his posture?

His lips twisted and he dropped his voice. "I am merely acting as befits my station." As the other guests found their seats he asked, "Do you like this house?"

Though she still felt the sting of her embarrassment, she could not stay angry with him for long. "I do!" she said with enthusiasm. "How is it that you have never talked of it?"

"Frankly, I have hardly been here in the last five years. I much prefer the country and there is so much to manage there. And I care little for the season."

"But you are here this year," she responded.

His defined jaw jutted out. "The pressure to marry is mounting. And with you here, I knew I could seek out interesting company if the need arose." He touched his nose "I should warn—"

His words were cut off as a footman introduced Stephen Manwaring and a short, pretty female she did not recognize.

Olivia threw a look of reproach at Jeremy who kept his eye firmly on the newly arrived guests.

"Manwaring!" he said, holding out his hand. "And this is your sister, I presume."

"Yes. Allow me to introduce Miss Vivienne Manwaring."

Olivia felt a stab of emotion as Jeremy caught hold of the ebony haired girl's hand. Her eyes were amber and lit up with excitement at his touch. Olivia's eyes shifted to Jeremy, and it was as if a lens had been moved, bringing him into sharper focus. His shiny, chestnut waves played around his collar and his broad shoulders dipped in an attractive manner under Miss Manwaring's gaze. Olivia supposed he was handsome, though she had never taken the time to consider it—he was just Jeremy. But the sister of

Mr. Manwaring was clearly impressed and dropped her chin in a most flirtatious fashion.

Olivia felt a jolt.

"Miss Deverell!" exclaimed Mr. Manwaring, forcing her to drag her attention from Jeremy. "I trust your ankle is better."

His face was full of earnest concern. "How kind of you to ask," she began, turning her best smile on him. "It is much better."

"And have you forgiven us for our little prank?" His lips curled and his brows followed and only a hard-hearted girl would not be able to forgive such contrition. "Of course, but I have cause for further anger since Lord Barclay did not tell me you would be one of the guests here this evening."

"He alone is at fault in this," Manwaring said, squeezing her hand.

"Indeed." She swung her gaze back to where Miss Manwaring and Jeremy were talking and was surprised to notice how fine his features were in comparison to the rugged profile of Mr. Manwaring.

After introductions were made all around, they were led to the dining room. Mr. Manwaring offered Olivia his arm, and she experienced a little stirring in her chest. As she noticed Jeremy conduct Miss Manwaring into the room, the emotion was batted away by something she could not quite define.

The dining room looked out onto a pretty garden filled with colorful blooms. The window had been propped open an inch and the sweet fragrance of the flowers floated in on a gentle evening breeze as the drapes fluttered.

She was positioned to sit next to Mr. Manwaring, and her aunt and mother were seated either side of Jeremy.

"I have been considering your question," Mr. Manwaring said as the soup was served.

"My question?" Her spoon stopped halfway to her mouth.

"Is knowledge innate?" He glanced sidelong at her.

He had remembered her question from the ball.

"And what is your conclusion?" she asked.

"I fear I may take the opposite stance from yourself. It is my opinion that a baby's brain can be considered as a fresh sheet of paper and that knowledge is gained through life by experience and teaching. I do not reject the notion that God can aid us in the getting of knowledge, but I am not of the school of thought that believes that the knowledge is already present and merely needs to be unlocked once mortal progress begins. What are your own thoughts?"

To be asked by a gentleman for her opinion on anything other than the food or the weather was so radical that she wanted to pinch herself.

"I have not yet drawn a conclusion," she admitted. "I am still considering the notion. Though I am leaning toward the same line of thinking as yourself. But when a great mind like Descartes proposes such a concept, it behooves us to give it careful consideration."

As the servants removed the soup bowls she asked him, "Tell me about your latest explorations. Did you find any new species?"

He turned his head toward her, a brow quirked and a smile of contentment on his lips that softened his harsh features.

For the rest of the meal, he told her in great detail about his studies in the South Pacific islands and she thrilled at being able to ask questions, which he answered with good grace, throughout the discourse. She quite forgot that other people were around the table until she heard her mother clear her throat.

"You are monopolizing Mr. Manwaring, Olivia. I am sure that others would care to hear about his exploits."

"My apologies," said Mr. Manwaring. "It is *I* who have monopolized your daughter's time."

Throughout dessert, he talked to the table at large but as soon as they were gathered together again in the drawing room, he sought her out and they continued their tête à tête.

Everything he said created more and more questions in her mind and not once was there any awkward silence. In fact, there did not seem enough time to discover everything she wanted to. When they were interrupted by his sister, she felt sad that their conversation was cut short.

"Stephen, I want to be introduced to Miss Deverell. Anyone who can endure hours of your ramblings is someone I want to get to know."

"Of course." There was no hint of irritation at his sister's request.

Vivienne bounced a curtsey to Olivia, who smiled back. No one could imagine that they were brother and sister.

"Do you not enjoy your brother's discoveries?" she asked.

"The first time hearing about them, perhaps," she said with good humor. "But I confess that I do tire of them by the sixth or seventh rendition."

A playful expression lit up Mr. Manwaring's eyes showing a softer side and Olivia felt her heart squeeze. Intelligent, progressive, *and* kind. A winning combination.

"And how are you enjoying your time here in London?" Olivia asked her.

"Very much, as long as it consists of balls and soirées. I am not one for intellectual evenings. Are you?"

"I cannot say I have ever been to one," admitted Olivia. "What are they like?"

"They are full of debate and exchange of ideas," said Mr. Manwaring with energy. "A group of academics and scholars come together to discuss any of one of a hundred topics."

"It sounds wonderful," said Olivia clasping her hands to her chest.

"Then I believe you are perfectly suited to be a companion of my brother," Miss Manwaring declared.

"Are you here with your family?" Olivia asked her.

Mr. Manwaring reached for his sister's hand. "I am guardian of my sister since my parents died."

Olivia's hands fell to her lap. "Oh, I am sorry to hear that. Please excuse my insensitivity."

"It has been many years now," he assured her. "I am really only here in town at my sister's request."

"Surely, the minds and sociality of London are an advantage to your career, are they not?" she asked.

"Indeed, they are, but I try to time my visits here outside the season for debutantes. I am not in the market for a wife, but my sister here, is now of age and I take it as my duty to allow her to parade herself like a peacock before all the fashionable young men."

"Stephen!" she chided, slapping him playfully on the arm.

"Is it not true?" he asked her.

She closed her eyes as if searching for a reservoir of patience. "I suppose so, but the way you frame the practice is indelicate."

One cheek curled showing a hidden dimple. "Then you concede my conclusions are accurate."

"Must everything be a debate with you, brother? You are thoroughly exhausting. I shall leave you to your erudite conversation and go in search of something tamer."

Miss Manwaring wandered across the room to Jeremy who had been watching them. Olivia was not sure she liked the way his eyes lit up at Miss Manwaring's approach.

"Where were we?" Mr. Manwaring asked, and Olivia was soon spellbound by his tales.

Chapter 8

Jeremy

Olivia's family was the first to leave. Aunt Frances needed her sleep, or so she said. Jeremy suspected that it was her sallow-faced daughter's doing. She had sat alone, neither engaging in conversations around her nor instigating her own. She had appeared thoroughly bored the entire evening. However, he was not unhappy that this put Olivia out of Manwaring's way. The intensity of their conversations was worrisome.

Jeremy now sat with his new friend and his delightful sister. Vivienne was pretty, engaging, and friendly. Everything a young man could hope for in a companion, but in comparison with Olivia, she did not reach the mark.

"I have a proposition that I need your opinion on," said Manwaring, causing Jeremy's heart to stutter. *Surely, he could not mean to propose after so short an acquaintance.*

"I am in need of a scribe."

Jeremy's anxiety burst. This was not what he had expected. "And you want me?"

"No, no! I am sure you have far more important things to do." He smoothed a thick eyebrow with a forefinger. "No, I merely want to ask your opinion on the wisdom of approaching Miss Deverell on the topic."

"You cannot be serious, Stephen!" declared Miss Manwaring. "She has come to London to find a husband not to be your scribe. The idea is preposterous!"

"Do you agree?" he asked Jeremy.

The idea of Olivia spending more intimate time with Manwaring was not encouraging and his first impulse was to dissuade him, but he knew in his heart that this was exactly the kind of work Olivia had dreamed of, and to deny her of the opportunity seemed petty. If he and Olivia were supposed to be together, it would all work out in the end.

"I believe that Olivia would jump at the chance. She flexes against the traditional constraints placed upon women and indeed, her eager brain deserves to be stretched."

Manwaring clapped his hands. "Splendid. Can you mention it to her? My usual chap has consumption and is unable to continue. I really need to get everything in order so that I can present my findings to the Royal Society."

"You really are going to make the attempt?" asked Jeremy. "It would make you the youngest scientist ever to be accepted, would it not?"

Manwaring played with his glass. "It would. I have great hopes of seeing my name among their ranks. It would also help in the funding of future explorations."

"I don't doubt it," said Jeremy. *He intends to leave again. Good!*

Miss Manwaring stood and extended her hand. "It has been a pleasure, Lord Barclay."

Both men stood and Jeremy took her delicate fingers. "The pleasure has been all mine."

She batted her eyelashes and Jeremy realized that she had set her cap at him.

When Jeremy arrived for tea at Aunt Frances' there was a great deal of comings and goings. As he reached the black front door, two sets of women were leaving and two more behind him arriving, meaning that the London season was in full swing.

As he entered the parlor, Olivia rolled her eyes.

"Too much of a good thing?" he whispered as he sat near her with a floral, bone china teacup and saucer.

"This is the very thing I detest about being a woman," she answered. "We are expected to make inane small talk with strangers and pretend to like it. And with people we have nothing in common with and whose dispositions are not at all complementary with our own." She set her own teacup on the occasional table at her side with such force that some tea spilled over and splashed onto the linen cloth.

"Then I may have some rather good news for you," he continued, his commission laying heavy on his heart.

A flash of hope shone from her eyes. "Please Jeremy! Save me from this fate."

He told her about Manwaring's proposition.

She almost squealed but swallowed it down and gripped the edge of her chair. "Really? He thinks me qualified for such a task?"

"You have made quite an impression on him, Olivia. And you are most certainly qualified. The only barrier I see is that your parents may not think it a suitable occupation for a young woman bent on finding a husband."

He watched as her eyes darted to her mother, currently engaged in discussing the weather for the umpteenth time with a mother and her rather plain daughter.

"Drat!" she exclaimed. "How in the world am I going to persuade Mother to allow it? And I can already envision the disapproval that will seep from Aunt Frances like damp from the basement."

"If you will allow me to couch the offer, I believe I can make them view it through the lens of..." He hesitated but had given the situation much thought. "Courtship."

Olivia jerked and her cheek sported a flash of color. "Courtship? Is that what Mr. Manwaring said? Is he hoping to court me?"

Was her reaction an indication that she was not ready to consider Manwaring as a suitor? He truly hoped so.

"I cannot speak to his intentions. He merely asked me to present the situation to you. He is in need of a good scribe and his current man is ill. But your mother and aunt don't need to know all that. How can they say no if I give the impression that Mr. Manwaring is showing affection for you in the only way he knows how? And I might mention that he intends to present his research to the Royal Society. That will be sure to impress your aunt."

Her head snapped up. "He does? That means that it is *really* important work. Work of great significance to the world at large. Oh, Jeremy! Can this be happening?"

She placed her hands over her nose as her eyes squeezed with silent jubilation and Jeremy's affection for her intensified.

The clock struck, indicating the end of visiting hours but Jeremy intended to stay to make his appeal to Mrs. Deverell.

"Jeremy," said Mrs. Deverell. "How nice it is to see old friends with whom one can relax. I find this whole tradition of visiting so tiring."

"I am glad that you feel at home with me," he began, "since I have come to ask a favor of you."

Mrs. Deverell tilted her head.

"You remember the great scientist, Mr. Manwaring, from my dinner, of course? Well, he has paid you the exceptional compliment of singling out your daughter for his attentions."

Understanding dawned across Mrs. Deverell's features.

"He has selected Olivia to act as scribe for him as he prepares his research for the Royal Society."

Olivia pursed her lips tight beside him, and her knuckles turned white.

Mrs. Deverell frowned. "How is acting as a scribe good for Olivia?"

Jeremy adjusted the knot at his throat and looked to Olivia for encouragement. "Mr. Manwaring is a man of science not of romance. He is on the cusp of fame with his findings and means to honor your daughter by offering her the chance to help him. Not only is this his way of courting, but he is offering Olivia the chance to be distinguished in her own right by the academic world."

Olivia's mother bit her lip. "You believe this man means to pay court to my daughter by asking her to scribe for him?"

Jeremy's heart twisted. "I do." As the words came out of his mouth he was flooded with misgivings. His love for Olivia and his desire to make her happy had been the only reason he was encouraging any of this, but the irony that his help could derail his own happiness was not lost on him.

Mrs. Deverell ran her finger around the edge of one of the many lace doilies. "And there will be a chaperone?"

"But of course! His sister will be there, though she will take no part in the exercise. And servants. It will all be very proper." For the third time, fate had offered him the chance to hinder the whole endeavor, and the devil on his shoulder was shouting in his ear to do just that.

"I shall have to discuss it with Mr. Deverell of course," she said, patting the lace on her bonnet. "But I see what you are saying, Jeremy."

Olivia's whole countenance rose but for once she kept her own counsel. It gave him some degree of happiness to see how much this opportunity gave her pleasure.

Mrs. Deverell left the room leaving the two of them behind. The sun from the window was dancing over Olivia's hair, emphasizing the golden strands. He had to ball his fists to keep from reaching out to touch them.

As soon as her mother's footsteps retreated, Olivia twirled around causing her ribbons to fly out to the side. "I cannot believe that things have come to such a happy pass!" she declared. "Not five minutes ago, I would never have believed that my mother would give her permission for such a thing as this. You are a talented persuader, Jeremy."

He considered the bitter paradox of her words.

Chapter 9

Olivia

Mr. Manwaring had taken rooms in a very respectable and spacious house. It was more of an apartment with an ample reception room boasting high ceilings decorated with plaster carvings and tall windows. Vivienne had come to collect Olivia from her aunt's house and she had chattered about girlish things all the way.

Nerves jangled in Olivia's stomach along with a healthy dose of excitement as Mr. Manwaring received them. He was dressed less formally, and his manner was all ease and familiarity. She was again struck by the sharp ruggedness of his features.

"Miss Deverell," he said, taking her hand. "You know not how much you will be helping me by performing this service. I have been stuck since my man became ill, and I am facing a deadline for the submission of my work if I am to be considered for the Society this year." His enthusiasm elevated his looks and Olivia felt a strange feeling start to grow in her stomach.

"I only hope I can live up to your lofty expectations," she responded.

"I have no doubt that you can. Come! Let me show you my study."

"Stephen!" cried Vivienne. "She has just this minute arrived. Give the poor girl a chance to catch her breath."

"Oh no!" responded Olivia. "I am anxious to begin."

Manwaring sent his sister a look that could only be described as triumphant and led the way to the study.

The room had a large window, but the curtains were mostly pulled, obscuring the light. He strode over and

55

pulled the fabric back, sending streams of summer sunlight in and revealing piles of leather-bound books that she supposed were his diaries.

She ran a finger over the top of one of the nearest stacks.

Manwaring gestured with his hand. "These are the books I filled on my latest adventure. Conditions were primitive and I was often scrawling notes on my knees for want of a desk. And there was so much to behold that I wrote faster than was judicious. Even I have a hard time deciphering what I wrote."

She opened a book and witnessed the messy handwriting he spoke of.

"Furthermore, I often used a kind of personal shorthand to remind myself of things to elaborate on when I got home." He clicked his heels. "This is what I propose. I will decode and dictate from these many volumes, while you write script neatly in a large manual that will be presented to the Royal Society." He grabbed a large, leather-bound book of parchment with a handle on the spine. He opened it and let her see the recording that had been done thus far.

The script was immaculate, conducted with a metal nib, with beautiful round letters and flowing tails. She hoped she could make hers half so nice.

"Are you ready?" he asked, his brows disappearing into the coarse curls of his head.

He indicated a plain desk that had been built with function in mind and pulled out a plain chair. He then presented her with an impressive pen with a gold nib and a bottle of Indian ink.

She scooted in the chair and placed her feet firmly on the ground, dipping the nib in the ink and holding the pen up, ready to write.

Mr. Manwaring spoke in a smooth, slow manner that gave her plenty of time to put the words on the parchment. The nib flowed effortlessly across the shiny surface and the cursive letters appeared beneath her hand. The instrument was so superior to a quill that she couldn't help but be impressed with the quality of the writing it produced.

For hours she wrote about the many plants and curious animals he had discovered until her hand began to cramp.

She gripped the offending appendage with her left hand as Manwaring continued his dictation without looking up.

"Excuse me," she said. "I shall need to rest for a while."

His brows knitted until he glanced at the grandfather clock. "Good gracious! Three hours have passed. Please excuse my enthusiasm for the subject, Miss Deverell. I have not even offered you a drink or a morsel to eat."

"The time has flown for me too," she said. "I am learning so much and would continue without a murmur were it not for my hand complaining."

At that very moment, Vivienne entered with lemonade on a tray.

"Brother, you are a hard taskmaster. Poor Miss Deverell will never want to return. I took the liberty of bringing some refreshment."

"Oh no," began Olivia. "I have scarcely ever enjoyed myself as much."

"Then you are a curious creature!" she declared. She brought a tall glass with the yellow liquid over to Olivia who drank deeply, surprised at her thirst.

"You must have some too, Stephen."

She tutted and explained, "Stephen has a habit of forgetting to eat or drink when he is engaged in his work. That is why he needs me." She shot a look at Olivia. "But when I marry, he will need to secure a wife to replace me."

Olivia felt uncomfortable at the talk of marriage. She had only just met Mr. Manwaring and it seemed presumptuous. She ducked her head and drank more lemonade.

"I shall not have time for a wife," he responded, "as I have plans to travel to the southern hemisphere, during the winter here, on another exploration."

Olivia was surprised that she felt disappointed.

He walked over to take a look at her work as she moved aside. "Adequate," he murmured as he looked.

Vivienne cast worried eyes at Olivia. "I am sure that Miss Deverell's work is more than adequate," she protested.

Manwaring looked up, his lips parted. "'Adequate' is high praise," he asserted. "It is all I ask."

Olivia hoped that meant that her work was satisfactory.

Her mother had given her permission to scribe three times a week for a maximum of four hours per session and that time was fast closing. Should she mention it? As a man of learning she was impressed that his subject so consumed him that he lost track of time, but her mother would not be understanding if she were late. Though Jeremy had succeeded in convincing Mrs. Deverell that the time spent with Mr. Manwaring would be like courting, her mother was not interested in putting all their eggs in one basket at this early stage of the season. There were balls and dinners to attend almost every evening.

"I shall call the carriage for Miss Deverell and escort her home," Vivienne declared.

"Is it time already?" Mr. Manwaring asked.

"It is, and if you anger Miss Deverell's mother by taking advantage, she will withdraw her permission and you will be out of a scribe again."

He leaned back in his chair and downed the rest of his lemonade then smiled at Olivia and it was as if a light went on inside her.

"I can't lose her."

A warmth began to spread in her chest.

"I am on a deadline."

Chapter 10
Jeremy

Jeremy had spent an entire afternoon walking around and around the British Museum. Olivia was anxious to see the exhibits so that she might discuss her findings with Stephen Manwaring. She had examined every display and read the accompanying literature. Her mother had accompanied them for propriety's sake but soon tired of the exhibitions and found herself a comfortable bench.

Now, as he sat in a box with Olivia's family in the King's Theatre waiting for the opera to begin, his arches ached. He had only succeeded in convincing Olivia to leave when she had begun to limp. Thankfully, their entertainment this evening was not a ball, and she was able to rest.

Olivia was sitting at the front of the box on display like flowers in a market, so that any eligible bachelor might examine her thoroughly with his opera glasses. He found the practice demeaning and hard to swallow. Tonight, she wore a delicate gown of the lightest blue that complemented her creamy skin tone and light hair. The tiniest ringlets had escaped her bun and formed a garland that graced her neck. He had not believed she could look any prettier than she had the day of the first ball, but a skilled hairdresser had artfully bound a white ribbon around her head, proving him wrong. He sat behind her, content to contemplate her hair and shoulders.

"Oh, there is Mr. Manwaring!" she cried, pointing. He leaned over and saw Vivienne and Stephen finding their seats below. When Manwaring had settled, he looked around, and seeing Olivia, raised a hand. Jeremy sat back. Manwaring's effect on Olivia was disconcerting, but he had not really witnessed an indication that she was affecting the scientist in any romantic way. At least he hoped not.

"This is my first opera!" said Olivia for the fifth time, turning to him, her eyes shining. He smiled and nodded as she went back to scanning the crowd.

Over the time she had been in town, he had observed more than one young man regarding her with interest, but she seemed oblivious. Her interest was all in Stephen Manwaring.

The conductor hit his music stand with his baton and the musicians readied their instruments as the curtain rose.

For the next sixty minutes he studied Olivia as she was spellbound by the opera, hardly moving a muscle. Though her sister Julia was the great musician of the family, the whole Deverell clan appreciated the art form wholeheartedly. His own appreciation was lacking; he found the high notes painful to his ears and preferred the symphony. But going to the opera was expected and besides, he could spend the time with Olivia.

However, by the time the interval started, he was ready to move his limbs.

"I am going in search of a drink. Anyone else want to come?" he asked the members of the box in general.

"Me!" said Olivia, getting to her feet. He proffered her his arm and they descended the staircase. Before they had reached the floor, she was pointing to Manwaring again and waving to catch his attention.

"Mr. Manwaring, how do you like the opera tonight?" she asked, looking up at him with an esteem that caused Jeremy to feel a tightness in his chest.

A sheepish look flashed across his heavy features. "Is it bad manners to admit that I am only here to accompany my sister?"

"The arias do not lift your soul, then?" she persisted.

"I could lie and tell you what you want to hear," he said. "But I shall not sport with your intelligence, Miss Deverell. They set my teeth on edge."

Vivienne laughed. "You are such a barbarian, brother!" she cried. "What about you?" she asked, turning the full force of her smile on Jeremy. Two ringlets hugged the side of her neck and jewels sparkled in her hair and ears. She was very pretty.

Jeremy gripped his chin. "Would it disappoint you to know that my own feelings are in line with your brother's?"

"Ahh!" she exclaimed. "I fear that without the fairer sex, the male population would regress to become wild and coarse boors. Don't you agree, Olivia?"

Olivia huffed. "I am sure I don't know," she replied, regarding the pair of them. "Perhaps most men are more cultured than these two specimens."

Miss Manwaring chuckled and flicked open her fan, hiding all but her eyes that were directed at him. "It is rather stuffy in here. Won't you all accompany me outside for some fresh air?" She held her elbow up for Olivia and the men followed.

"I see that the sprain is still affecting Miss Deverell," said Manwaring as Olivia's gait leaned a little.

"It is due to a childhood accident," said Jeremy, without thinking, regretting the words as soon as they were out of his mouth. Olivia would not thank him for divulging this.

"Indeed?" said Manwaring. "Is she lame?"

Jeremy knew he would need to choose his words carefully to make amends. "I would not say that. She fell from a tree when she was eleven years old and kept it from her parents. I fear it fractured and was never set properly. Most of the time it is barely noticeable but if she has done a lot of walking or dancing, or it is damp, it bothers her."

He saw with alarm that Manwaring's eyes were narrowed.

"We spent many hours at the British Museum today and so it aches a little. She was determined to learn as much as she could to impress you." He hoped the reason for her limp would distract him from the affliction itself.

"Such an imperfection will harm her chances at marriage, I presume."

The slight hit Jeremy as hard as if the comment had been launched at him personally.

"Imperfection you call it?" His voice was louder than he intended and had risen in pitch. "I call it character. It reminds me of her daring spirit."

Manwaring shook his head. "Not that I am interested in securing a wife, but if I was, I should need someone who can manage the rough territory of the distant lands I visit, not a person with any kind of impediment."

Jeremy could feel the heat rising in his blood. How dare he criticize Olivia! He took a moment before responding. "There is more of value in that woman than in all the rest of the women here tonight combined. I would not cast her aside for such a small injury."

Manwaring was not impressed with Jeremy's defense. "It is a shame, for I was beginning to become fond of your little friend."

Anger flashed in Jeremy's mind, and he bit his tongue for fear of offending the eminent man. He pushed open the door to the opera house before the attendant could do it, with more force than necessary. The two young women were already strolling in the cool, night air.

"Lord Barclay," said Miss Manwaring, turning and addressing Jeremy. "I should deem it a great favor if you were to take my arm. Stephen, attend to Miss Deverell."

Her grip on his arm was tight and she leaned her head so close to his that her hair tickled his cheek. "You do not like the opera, then?" she said, a coy smile playing around her rosy lips.

"I prefer the symphony," he said, checking over his shoulder, worried that Manwaring would say something to offend Olivia.

Miss Manwaring ran a gloved hand down his arm. "Ah, the symphony. I am a great lover of the orchestra too, but I love the pageantry of the opera."

"It has no appeal for me, but I am happy to accompany whomever, if it gives them pleasure." As he looked back, he saw the smile drop from Olivia's face and her eyes tumble to her feet. He slowed his step so that he might eavesdrop on their conversation.

"It is not so very uncomfortable," he heard her say. "I have merely over-used it today. All will be better tomorrow."

His heart sunk and he felt deep regret that he had mistakenly shared her secret.

"I should not be able to accomplish my life's work with such a handicap," Manwaring commented, as Olivia's shoulders drooped farther.

"Lord Barclay," reprimanded Vivienne. "Did you not hear what I just said?"

The truth was he had not. In spite of her good looks, she could not hold a candle to the worth of Olivia and he felt the urge to throw off her arm and run to Olivia's assistance.

He refrained and the clock struck, indicating that it was time to return. They retraced their steps and after seeing Miss Manwaring to her seat, he took Olivia's arm to climb the stairs to their box.

"What has been your favorite part of the drama so far?" he asked, hoping to bring the joy back to her countenance.

"Jeremy, why did you tell Mr. Manwaring about my ankle?" she asked, ignoring his question.

It was as if she had slapped his cheek. "He noticed your limp and thought it was from spraining your ankle at the ball. I let out your secret before I realized. Can you forgive me?"

She raised hurt eyes. "Though I would rather he did not know, that no one knew, you and I are old and dear friends and of course, I freely forgive you. What hurts is Mr. Manwaring's prejudice against such things."

"What did he say?" Jeremy asked.

"He merely rejoiced in his own fortune at not having such a burden as it would prevent him from his explorations. His meaning was clear. He thinks less of me because I am broken."

Jeremy halted and took her by the shoulders. "You are *not* broken, Olivia, and any man that thinks such is not worth your time."

She contemplated him with glassy eyes and a trembling lip. The urge to kiss her was almost more than he could bear. She wiped a tear that spilled over.

"Thank you," she murmured. "You always make me feel better." And leaning, she kissed him on the cheek.

"I hope my idiocy has not spoiled your enjoyment of the opera."

"No, no," she said as they opened the door to the box, but he knew it was a lie.

Chapter 11

Olivia

Olivia slid her hand down the smooth, oak banister of the grand staircase on her way to the breakfast room. They had returned late from the opera, and she had not been able to sleep right away. The conversation with Mr. Manwaring had played over and over in her mind. As a consequence, she was late to breakfast. Her slippered feet padded across the black and white tile toward the sound of muffled voices. As she stood outside the door, the smell of fried potatoes wafted under the door and her hungry stomach growled with anticipation.

"Olivia," said her aunt, drawing out the syllables. "I thought you must have gone out early." Aunt Frances eyed the clock on the wall, her lips puckered in disapproval.

"My apologies, Aunt," she said, sweeping her gown under her as she sat on the chair. "I did not sleep well last night."

"Hmmm," replied her aunt.

"She's here now," said her mother, pushing the curls on her neck with nervous fingers. "No harm done, sister."

Olivia checked her aunt's reaction. She tried to love her mother's sister, but the woman made it so difficult. She always caused the Deverells to feel like poor relations and it irked Olivia. And she was in no mood to be pleasant this morning.

A footman appeared at her elbow with the seasoned potatoes and laid fragrant brown, fried slices onto her plate. Another footman offered her eggs which he piled high. In spite of her mood, she realized she was hungry and raised a fork. Her aunt coughed.

"Yes?" said Olivia.

"I just wanted to remind you that a lady takes small bites, niece."

Olivia bit her tongue, taking a moment before remarking, "Of course, Aunt. I thank you." She cut her eyes over to her mother who twitched an eyebrow.

"And I feel it my duty as a resident of London and an intimate member of the social elite to point out that it will be difficult to secure the affection of a young man with Lord Barclay always in the wings."

Olivia dropped the fork and it clattered against the china plate. "Lord Barclay is my best friend," she said through gritted teeth.

"There you go," said her aunt, flicking her napkin and smoothing it onto her skirts. "Whoever heard of a young lady with a *man* for a friend. It is just not done."

"Jeremy is more intelligent than most of the young men I have encountered in London thus far. None of them can even solve my riddle before a dance ends."

"Riddle?" Her aunt glared over glasses that were perched on the end of her generous nose.

"Yes, I find it a useful way to test the intellect of my partners."

"A test?" Her aunt put down the correspondence she was reading. "That is no way to find a husband, child. What do you say, Georgina?"

She saw her mother lift her neck and shake her head slightly so that her curls wobbled.

"Olivia is not an empty-headed young lady, as so many are, and is in search of someone who can complement her wide-ranging interests." Her voice was clipped.

Aunt Frances narrowed her eyes to slits, criticism oozing. "I have always said that your girls are far too clever for their own good. Filling their heads with philosophy and politics. No man wants a wife who will argue with him."

"All my girls are peacemakers," said Mrs. Deverell in their defense and Olivia felt a rush of affection for her mother. It was not quite true, but she was happy that her mother said it anyway. She and Genevieve were always butting heads. "And they will be able to hold a rational conversation with their husbands just as Richard and I do. Don't you agree, darling?"

This last was addressed to Olivia's father who was nose deep in the morning paper. Olivia knew he had not the least idea what her mother was talking about.

"Hmmm," he replied, not even lowering the paper an inch.

Her mother was not to be deterred in the exoneration of her family. "We have spirited conversations around the table at dinner. What young man would not like that?"

Aunt Frances shook her considerable head. "I have never understood you, Georgina. I was happy to sit by Mama with my needlework and you always had to be doing."

Olivia looked down the table at her cousin Mary, who was staring into her plate.

"How dull the world would be if we were all alike," replied Mrs. Deverell, with some spirit.

"I suppose—"

Whatever her aunt supposed was halted by a footman announcing the arrival of Mary's sister, Theodora, with her children. Her aunt sailed from the room like a ship. Mary followed in her wake.

Olivia exhaled.

"Olivia, that was probably unwise," suggested her mother. "Please do not give your aunt any more ammunition against us."

"She is so formal, even when it is just the family," Olivia complained. "I am grateful that she has allowed us to stay, but she makes such demands of me. I do not like it."

"There, there," said her mother. She poured some water from a silver pitcher. "But she may have a point about Jeremy. It may suggest that you are a couple and dissuade other gentlemen."

Olivia rested her silverware across her plate. "Are you suggesting that I tell Jeremy he is not welcome anymore? Mother! He is like part of our family. I shall not do it!" She tempered her tone. "And besides, it has not dissuaded Mr. Manwaring." Her mother did not need to know his opinion of her limp if it helped her case.

Mrs. Deverell looked across the table at Olivia, sharply. "You believe he will propose?"

She must watch her words. "I cannot say for sure. He has honored me with the job of scribe and seems to value my opinion on things, but I would not say we have progressed to that point. He is, after all, an important man in his field, bent on making his name. I think finding a wife is of secondary importance to him at this juncture."

"Well, if that is the case, you cannot wait for him to be ready and waste your time in London. Your sisters are eager for their chance, which cannot be accomplished until you are engaged. It is time to search for someone else, I think. Tonight, at the Queen Charlotte ball you should dance with as many strangers as you possibly can. Men of the best quality will be in attendance."

Olivia snorted. "You make them sound like prize bulls, Mama."

"Don't be vulgar, darling. I mean it. Try to be as charming as you can. There are plenty of amiable, intelligent men in the world. You are a pretty girl who can win a man over with a winning smile and pretty conversation. No more riddles."

The forecourt of St. James's Palace was bustling with carriages, horses and debutantes. Though Olivia was bubbling over with uneasiness about being presented, it was her first visit to court, and she was soaking in every detail of the ancient, red palace. In truth, other than the impressive octagonal towers built by Henry VIII, she was surprised how small and low the building was compared to other great homes she had been to. But its history— *that* was notable, and she knew that somewhere the heart of Queen Mary I was buried. She suppressed a shudder.

The air was rife with horse dung and smoke as she and her family tiptoed across the cobblestones to enter the main doors.

It was a warm June evening, no need for capes, as they entered the grand foyer. The interior made up for what was lacking on the outside of the palace and Olivia gasped at the beautiful staircase with gold plated filigree railings that split halfway up, showcasing enormous paintings framed with wood in cream and blue. Two gold lamp posts with flickering candles, flanked the first step.

"The inside is just what a palace should be," Olivia whispered to her mother as they followed the crowd up the stairs.

She had spent the time after lunch writing for Mr. Manwaring but left early to start her toilette for the ball. The conversation from the previous evening had dulled her enthusiasm for him and the season. She chafed at the fact that she had allowed her heart to admit him, and his criticism of her injury, his inference that it had left her a cripple, had hurt her pride. Following her parents, she pushed the memory of the depressing comment aside. This evening she would start with a clean slate, hold her tongue, and be on her best behavior.

Olivia wore a special gown for her presentation, and though she was not particularly interested in dresses, she had to admit to an uncharacteristic affection for this one. As she beheld herself in one of the mirrors on the stairs, she realized she might even be described as elegant.

Progress forward was slow, which gave her time to inspect the paintings and the general splendor. She knew that the palace contained a library and wondered if she would have occasion to sneak into it during the course of the evening.

At last, the massive serpentine of guests flowed into the ballroom and Olivia went up on her toes to see over the crowd. A little knot of nerves was growing in her stomach. Tonight's ball was of a great deal more consequence than the others. What if she fell in front of the queen or fell into the queen's birthday cake when she curtsied?

As she peered at the crowd, she could see that the room was replete with handsome gentlemen. Fresh from the hurt of Mr. Manwaring's criticism, she was more than open to considering other possibilities. Perhaps, in spite of her fears to the contrary, there was an intelligent and handsome young man here who could pique her interest…if she could just survive her presentation to the queen.

Her father had stopped to talk to an acquaintance when she heard her name.

Jeremy!

"Olivia! Allow me to introduce you to Felix Armstrong."

Turning, Olivia beheld a tall, thin man with a weak chin. She flicked her gaze to Jeremy.

"Mr. Armstrong is a mathematician." The statement was declared with raised brows.

Olivia extended her hand for the young man to kiss. He stared at it for a second and then, as if remembering the social customs, took her hand. "Delighted to meet you, Miss Deverell. Lord Barclay has told me that we share an interest in academics."

She lowered her voice. "I confess that I do love mathematics, history, and philosophy but there are so few people who share my passion."

70

With its peculiar edges, Mr. Armstrong's face was far from traditionally handsome, but his eyes were sincere and filled with an eager earnestness.

"And even fewer of them are women, I find." His lips curled, producing a crooked smile.

She dipped her head, to hide her amusement. "Indeed."

"Perhaps you can add your name to Miss Deverell's dance card, Mr. Armstrong?" suggested Jeremy.

At this, the said Mr. Armstrong faltered, the awkward smile sliding from his face like rain from a window. "Ahh, I fear that my skills do not run to dancing, Miss Deverell."

"And yet you are at a ball," Olivia responded.

His lips tightened and his long nose trembled. "I am sure that a person as lovely and young as yourself has never had the experience of testy relatives. Relatives who have no compunction against informing one that you have become a burden to society in your single state." The meandering smile crept back.

"Oh, but you are mistaken Mr. Armstrong! It is for that very reason that I am in London for my season," she shot back. "At least two of my three younger sisters are eager to come out, and practically commanded me to find a husband."

"Then you know exactly to what I refer." His slight hand went to the crisp, white knot at his neck. "I have come to this ball at the insistence of my grandmother, who is also my guardian. But you must believe me when I say that if I were forced to dance, I should ostracize all the young ladies with my clumsiness." He opened his mouth and a laugh, like the bray of a donkey escaped. Olivia resisted the urge to look at Jeremy.

"But I should be honored to take supper with you." Vulnerability flashed across his elongated face.

Though she felt no spark of connection, she sensed that it had taken some effort to ask her, and she reasoned that he would be interesting to talk to. "I accept your kind offer," replied Olivia. "Shall we say ten o' clock?"

"Olivia! What is keeping you?" Her mother's tone was full of impatience as she looked Mr. Armstrong up and down. "Oh, Jeremy! It is you that has kept her."

"Guilty, ma'am," he said with some humor. "Allow me to introduce Mr. Armstrong."

Her mother's smile faded into a grimace. It was obvious she did not quite approve of Mr. Armstrong's appearance.

"Enchanted," she breathed.

This time, Mr. Armstrong was ready for the social expectations and took her mother's hand placing a fish-like kiss upon it.

Her mother frowned.

"Mr. Armstrong has kindly agreed to accompany me to supper," Olivia said.

"Indeed. How kind."

Mr. Armstrong bowed and slipped away allowing other men to approach and add their names to Olivia's dance card. In order to save her ankle, she had placed a line through every other set, and to please her family she had agreed to speak only of acceptable topics, though how she would find out a young man's character with such vacuous words she did not know.

The first few men she danced with were as empty headed as she had imagined, but she tried to enjoy the dances as entertainment in themselves. As she bobbed and swayed, she found herself scanning the crowd for Mr. Manwaring, though she hated herself for it.

She had been tight-lipped and all efficiency that afternoon as she scribed for him and though it had irked her that he had been blind to the coolness in her bearing, she could not help hoping to see him. His callous comment the night of the opera had certainly thrown a wedge between them of which he seemed oblivious. At the end of their writing session, he had informed her that he would be in attendance at the Queen Charlotte Ball that evening, with his sister.

And now she could not help herself.

At length she spotted Vivienne in another quadrille and her search for Mr. Manwaring intensified. Though her ardor for him had waned, she had to admit that her feelings for him were still smoldering embers. She admired his work and ambition and there was a charisma that could not be denied.

But she would not seek him out.

After several more sets, a courtier announced that the time had come to introduce the debutantes and nerves shot through her. She was not accustomed to being the center of attention and the caliber of the people present merely served to increase the pressure.

Each young woman to be presented was announced with great pomp and walked across the floor to be recognized by the queen. Girls of every size and shape went through the ceremony as the other guests looked on.

When her own name was announced, Olivia felt a jolt of pure fear. All was well as she walked with tiny, practiced steps across the floor, but as she placed her foot on the small stairs to the dais where stood the queen, her bad ankle foundered, and with a sickening sense of horror she felt herself crumple to the floor in a puff of silk and ribbons. A crescendo of concerned gasps filled the silence, increasing her humiliation. She quickly pushed herself up and placed a hand to her hot cheek, keeping her eye firmly on the queen whose expression, she was relieved to see, was one of pure sympathy.

After she curtsied and the next name was called, Olivia fled from the room, desperate for escape from the scene of her disgrace. As she pushed through the crowd, she heard a familiar voice.

"I have it on good authority that Miss Olivia Deverell is lame. Not many men would be willing to take on an imperfect girl like that for a wife."

It was Mr. Manwaring.

Chapter 12
Jeremy

Jeremy was close on Olivia's heels.

As she weaved rapidly through the crowd he lost sight of her, but as he left the ballroom, he spotted her running down a long, red carpeted corridor. Hurrying to catch up, he eventually found her huddled on a bench in an obscure corner. She looked up, eyes frantic like a cornered rabbit.

"Oh, it's just you. Please go away." Her face shone with hot tears, and she hung her head again, her shoulders shaking. He ignored her request and sunk down on his haunches, peering up from beneath.

She squeezed her eyes tight. "Let me wallow in my humiliation alone."

"I am sure you are not the first debutante to lose her footing, nor will you be the last," he assured her. "Who among us has not fallen at some point in their life? I have even heard that one of the royal princesses had such an incident."

A warm tear splashed onto his hand.

"It is not only the fall," she spluttered.

He shifted his feet to get better balance. "But what else could cause such agony?"

She opened eyes laced with red, lines of distress working their way across her forehead. "It is Mr. Manwaring. He has labeled me a cripple before all society and warned the gentlemen against me."

"Surely not!" His heart quickened with fury.

"I heard him with my own ears, Jeremy. He has greatly deceived me. I thought he was my friend." She wiped her tears. "I am ruined."

He reached out to brush a tear away with his thumb and the feel of her skin triggered a warmth in his own. "The cad! Most ungentlemanly behavior! Manwaring is not worth your time, Olivia. We have both been deceived in his character, and I fear he is married to his work. He will end up an old, lonely man, pottering amongst his specimens."

Her head fell back. "How can I return to the ball now? I will never be able to hold my head up in polite society again," she moaned.

He reached for her hand, stroking the fingers with his to soothe her. She stopped her tears and looked at him, her damp face full of confusion. A force outside his will tugged his chin, lifting his face to hers so that their lips were mere inches apart, white hot energy crackling between them.

"I—" he murmured.

Almost imperceptibly she moved forward, her trembling lips so close he could feel their energy.

His heart leapt to his throat. Was this an invitation? He leaned closer, eyes shutting—

"There you are!" Vivienne appeared, out of breath.

Jeremy rolled back and sprung up like a coiled wire. "Miss Manwaring! What are you doing here?"

"I saw what happened. My dear, I am so sorry," she said, addressing Olivia. "It could have happened to anyone. I came to offer some sisterly sympathy."

The tears began again in earnest, but Olivia was looking at him now.

Vivienne sat down beside Olivia and pulled her head onto her shoulder, also staring at Jeremy.

He looked back and forth between the two women.

Olivia so familiar and dear. Olivia who had blossomed into a handsome woman this year. Olivia who viewed him as a brother. But had she been about to accept his kiss? The emotions in his chest were swirling like a tornado, and he wiped a hand across his mouth.

His eyes went to Miss Manwaring. So petite and feminine. So conventionally pretty. So interested in unimportant things. So unable to amuse him with clever debate. He felt no fire when he conversed with her.

He paced to burn off the energy of crushing disappointment.

"Lord Barclay, your compassion is to be admired but do not worry yourself. I am here now."

The urge to yell that her brother had excoriated Olivia in a public place rose like bile in his throat, and only with the utmost self-control was he able to desist. Instead, after several minutes his voice shook as he said, "I make it my business to defend my friends in their distress."

"That is most honorable," Miss Manwaring replied, a half-smile on her lips, eyes staring deeply into his.

He turned his head.

"I just want to go home," said Olivia quietly.

"I shall go in search of your parents," he offered and began to walk away.

"Jeremy." His name on her lips caused him to stop in his tracks.

"Thank you."

Chapter 13

Olivia

Two missives the following day caused opposite emotions in Olivia's breast.

The first, a letter from her sister Julia, announced that her mother and father had given permission for her to come to town for a few days. This gave Olivia great solace. Of all her sisters, she was closest to Julia and welcomed her visit as an outlet for the distress and humiliation she had experienced since the debacle at the Queen Charlotte Ball.

The second was a message to her parents from Jeremy that he had been called back to his estate by some emergency, that caused a case of melancholy to settle over her.

Her sister Julia was to arrive that evening, and Olivia yearned for her appearance throughout the day, keeping to her room with a book she pretended to read in order to avoid her family.

She was supposed to have gone that afternoon to work for Mr. Manwaring but sent a curt note that she was unwell. To her knowledge, Mr. Manwaring was unaware that she had overheard his defamation of her and hoped he would view her embarrassing clumsiness as the real cause for staying away.

Never is time so long as when one is wishing it away, and such was the case for Olivia. The hours dragged on, the minutes mocked, and even the seconds seemed to delay. She refused all food until by dinner time her stomach complained so loudly and she was forced to ask for a supper tray.

Every sound of carriages in the street caused her ears to perk, but since London was a busy city the sounds of horses and carriage wheels was steady. At length, the constant anticipation caused a headache.

Finally, at ten minutes past eight, the clack of hooves slowed near the curb. She pulled back her bedroom curtains delighted to see her sister alight from the carriage and stretch her back. Her first instinct was to fly down the stairs into her sister's embrace but she still feared the pity in the faces of her relatives and began to pace instead.

Excited voices of welcome floated up from the foyer and Olivia's eagerness caused her to clench her fists so hard that the nails made imprints in her palms.

A knock at her door caused her to gasp but it was merely the servants bringing up Julia's luggage and she fell back on her bed.

Another twenty minutes passed before the familiar step of her sister was heard in the hallway and she had scarcely entered when Olivia flung her arms around her neck, almost knocking her down.

"Olivia, to what do I owe such an outpouring of sisterly love? Do you not like London and its diversions?"

"Oh, Sister! Did Mama not tell you? I have recently been made a laughingstock in more ways than one in the eyes of high society, and I want nothing more than to flee from it."

Julia pushed back to inspect her sister's eyes. "But how can that be? You exaggerate, surely?"

"I wish that were the case," began Olivia, and laid out the whole sorry tale in detail.

"This Mr. Manwaring? Who is he to us?" declared Julia. "What does it matter that he thinks ill of you? Only a stupid man would cast off a woman because of a slight limp. What nonsense!"

For the first time since her fall, Olivia felt a smile pull at her lips as her sister vociferously defended her honor.

"Oh, Julia it is so good to have you here as an ally."

Julia grabbed her hands. "But tell me more about Jeremy's part in the plot. You thought he might kiss you?"

"Had Mr. Manwaring's sister not arrived, I believe that our lips would have touched."

Julia quirked a brow. "And how do you feel about that?"

"I hardly know. Jeremy is my friend—has always been my friend, but…"

"Yes?" prodded her sister.

"I believed that he had developed feelings for Miss Manwaring. She makes no secret of her interest in him, and I thought he reciprocated her feelings."

"What makes you say that?" asked Julia, dragging her sister over to a pretty, taffeta couch that sat under the window.

"She is refined and pretty in a way I can never hope to be. What man would *not* be interested in her in comparison to an argumentative cripple like me?"

"I forbid you to use that word!" cried Julia. "You are no more a cripple than I am a dunce." She smoothed her skirt and looked sidelong at her sister. "In truth, I have long suspected a preference on Jeremy's part."

"For you?" Olivia's heart jumped into her throat.

Julia's lips flattened and she chuckled. "Perhaps *you* are the dunce! Not for me—for you, of course!"

Olivia pulled back and frowned. "What makes you say that?"

"He hides it well, but I have noticed him watching you when he thinks no one is paying attention. I have never mentioned it before because I know your feelings for him are platonic—but I wonder…is that still the case?" Olivia felt she was under the heat of the midday sun as her sister's dark blue eyes probed her own.

"Until yesterday I should have said yes, but Julia, I *wanted* him to kiss me. But it would ruin everything. And besides, I still think he may be in love with Miss Manwaring."

"What makes you say that?"

"He left in a great hurry today with the excuse that there was some problem at home on his estate. You may have passed him on the road without knowing it. Is that not evidence that he was merely caught up in the heat of the moment and already regrets his actions?"

Julia slapped her thigh. "It is evidence that he is called away by a legitimate problem on the estate. Do not sell yourself short, Olivia." She pulled her sister over to the dressing table and pushed her shoulders until she sat down. "See, you have improved greatly these last months."

Olivia stared at her reflection. She saw the same light hair, the same bluish eyes, but perhaps her cheeks had become a little more defined.

"Forget Mr. Manwaring," said Julia. "He is not worthy of you."

As she sat examining her own face, Olivia conjured up an image of Mr. Manwaring. He was not handsome, but he *was* going to distinguish himself in the world of science and he *did* favor her with pithy conversation and listened intently to her musings. Did such qualities make up for deficiencies in appearance?

"Now," declared Julia. "Let us go down and I shall play for you."

Olivia's bottom lip shrugged. "But I have not been seen in public since my mishap. How can I face anyone?"

"Like a Deverell!" cried Julia. "Hold your head high and defy anyone to mention your blunder."

Chapter 14

Jeremy

Jeremy had received an urgent letter from his mother telling him that she was ill. With her health always in the balance he thought it prudent to go home directly.

The long journey provided him plenty of time for reflection and to regain his composure. He was furious that Manwaring had maligned Olivia in such a public manner, and it was probably just as well to cool off his temper before addressing the matter, lest he end up in jail for battery.

An image of Olivia's quivering lips and tortured eyes would not leave his mind. How dare the man slander her so!

On the other hand, each time he recalled the tension as he and Olivia moved toward each other in that remote hallway, his heart caught in his chest. Now he knew that if she wouldn't have him, no other woman would do.

Upon arrival at home, he rushed up the stairs and demanded to be led to his mother.

He was surprised when instead of being taken to her bedchamber, he was ushered into her private parlor where she sat with her companion. The summer sun was pouring in, lighting her soft, brown hair like a flame of fire and he experienced the first inklings that he had been led on a wild goose chase.

His mother was in fine health.

An angelic smile spread over her face as he strode over to her favorite armchair, but he felt anger igniting in his chest at the wasted journey.

"Mother! You gave me to understand that you were critically ill," he scolded.

"I am! I miss you so much when you are gone that I lose my appetite." A naughty puppy could not have looked more contrite. He softened.

Taking her slight hand in his, he said, "I would have come home for a visit if you requested it. There is no need to be dramatic."

"But you are enjoying your time there far more than with me, I don't doubt. I had to make the reason compelling. Now, tell me all about it. Have you met a wife?"

Jeremy cast his gaze out the window, the tide of anger draining. "Perhaps."

His mother clapped her hands together. "Tell me about her."

He kept his eye trained on the birds swooping on the currents of air outside. "She is spirited and clever and more importantly, a person of substance."

"Is she pretty?"

He turned from the window to see that his mother's face was brimming with hope from under her lace cap.

"More than pretty, Mother. She is beautiful."

The dowager clasped her fists under her chin. "And when shall I meet her?"

He looked out the window again and saw a family of deer feeding in the meadow. "I have not made a declaration yet. I have to be sure she feels the same. Until then I shall not propose." He wagged his finger. "You have brought me from that very purpose."

Disappointment bloomed across his mother's features much as it must have done on his when Vivienne Manwaring appeared in the hallway at the palace. "Then do it soon."

"Romance is like a fine wine—if you hurry it, you may end up with something more approaching vinegar."

His mother's chest rose, and a ragged sigh escaped. "I suppose you are right. I just long for grandchildren to fill this home. I can almost hear them laughing sometimes. I daresay that makes me appear to be mad, but they are so real in my imagination."

His own desire to be married was just as strong and he recognized the truth of what his mother was saying. He patted her hand. "All in good time," he murmured.

Rather than turn tail and leave for London immediately, he spent a day riding the pastures of the estate and seeking peace about the course of action he was about to take. If he made a declaration and Olivia refused him, the longstanding friendship they had enjoyed would be destroyed. Was he prepared for that outcome? Yes, because that moment in the palace hallway had been a light in the dark and he thought it was now worth the risk.

He was of an age to marry, and it was what his heart truly yearned for. Whenever he had to leave Olivia, he felt the loss. To have her as his wife, to never have to be parted from her, was all he wanted, and the events of the past weeks had proved that to him more than ever.

He had fooled himself if he thought he was reconciled to her marrying someone else. If that happened, he would have to run away to South America, though it would break his mother's heart. The very thought of having to pretend to like her husband at dinner parties and soirées was his idea of purgatory. He would not put himself through it.

He stopped the horse and sat in his saddle looking across his estate. The sun was hidden behind the clouds as his eyes swept the beloved landscape. But he would readily sacrifice it if he could not have her; hire some qualified, trusted land manager to run it.

He turned the horse around with a great ache in his heart, not sure whether it was for the girl or the land.

Chapter 15

Olivia

Green Park was bustling with nobility on this sunny, summer afternoon. Though she had much rather stay inside, Julia's energy and excitement to be in the city could not be ignored and all the visiting Deverells, including Olivia, surveyed the crowd from the comfort of Aunt Frances's open carriage.

A carefully placed fan hid her face, allowing Olivia to remain incognito and cradle her bruised ego. On the other hand, Julia had to be reprimanded to watch her manners as she twisted and turned in her seat, transported by the ornate dresses and hats.

"Dash it all! Is that not Miss Manwaring?" asked Mrs. Deverell as they moved slowly along the path. Olivia dared not look up.

"Please do not attract her attention," pleaded Olivia, "she will only add to my shame."

However, fate was not a friend today and before they could trot by unnoticed, Miss Manwaring had waved and moved toward the carriage. To ignore her now would be the height of bad manners and simply could not be done— even Olivia understood this.

How she wished she had stood her ground and stayed at home under some pretense, but Julia had convinced her that the chance of seeing an acquaintance in the crowded arena was highly unlikely.

A whirling dervish of emotions filled Olivia's chest as Vivienne approached.

"How do you do?" she said as she reached the coach. "And who is this charming young woman?"

"Allow me to present my younger daughter, Julia," explained Mrs. Deverell. "She is here for a few days."

"Ah, then I have heard about you." She nodded to Olivia. "Your sister has been singing your praises."

Julia beamed with pleasure.

"Would you care to take a turn with me?" Miss Manwaring addressed her question to the   whole carriage.

"It is rather too hot for me," declared Mrs. Deverell. "But perhaps…?"

Her mother had witnessed Olivia's unfortunate fall at the ball and consequent request to leave, but she was ignorant of Mr. Manwaring's treachery. However, Mrs. Deverell was sensitive enough to appreciate how distressing the incident had been on its own merits and Olivia was grateful that she appeared intent on protecting her feelings until she felt up to going out in public again.

Olivia nudged her sister in the ribs.

"Oh yes! I should love to." Julia stood and the servant pulled out the step.

Miss Manwaring took her by the arm, under the shade of her parasol. "Shall we say fifteen minutes, then?"

The carriage pulled away to make a circle and Olivia let out the breath she was holding. Would she ever live her societal faux pas down? Her first instinct last night had been to demand to go back to Worcester Park but her mother had persuaded her that memories were fickle and that her fall had not been so bad as she thought and besides, her sister was to arrive.

Lest they were spotted by another acquaintance, Olivia held the fan higher. This idea to take some air in the park had certainly lost its luster.

Julia had returned to the carriage her solemn eyes nervous with news, but she had held her tongue until they were back in the bedroom they shared.

"You are right," Julia began, once they were alone. "Miss Manwaring spent the whole fifteen minutes talking about Jeremy. She never once mentioned your unfortunate accident."

Olivia flung her arm against the wall and rested her head on it. "I finally see Jeremy as a suitor, and realize his…value, and he is lost to me."

"You think you love him, then?" asked Julia, gripping her sister's other arm.

Eyes wet with tears, Olivia lifted her head. "Since he left, I feel that a part of me is missing. Is not that love? But how can I compete with Miss Manwaring? I am sure that *she* does not argue at breakfast, lunch, and dinner. And I am confident that she is content to keep house and smile at visitors." She clung to her sister. "Oh Julia! I fear that I am too late."

Instead of encouragement her sister's face was clouded with doubt. "She certainly felt that Jeremy had encouraged her and that he might make a request of her brother to begin a formal courtship."

Olivia sunk to the bed. "My life is over."

So distraught was Olivia at the thought of Miss Manwaring as Jeremy's wife, that she begged to be excused from tea that afternoon. The very idea of pretense that all was well while she felt so desperate, was simply more than she could bear.

However, when Julia returned to the room, she wished she had gone.

"Jeremy came!" Julia cried before the door had even half closed.

"What?" she cried, jumping up from the couch, her hands to her mouth. "Why didn't you send a maid to tell me? I thought he was still in Worcestershire."

"So did we all, but he said that the matter was not so pressing as he had been led to believe and returned to town this morning. And he did not stay long. I have come up directly after visiting was over."

Olivia's stomach twisted with anticipation. "And did he talk of Miss Manwaring?"

Julia, her golden hair braided around a discreet bun, paced the floor. "I asked about his journey, of course, and then since we are more than acquaintances, I asked him directly about her." She stopped to face her sister, blue eyes filled with pride that she had been so daring.

Olivia both praised and cursed her for she cringed at the prospect she was about to hear news that would dash her hopes forever.

Julia grabbed her sister's hands and danced a jig. "He was most forceful in his denials. He declared that he had never been partial to Miss Manwaring, that all the pursuit was from her side."

A blanket a relief wrapped itself around Olivia and the little flame of hope that still burned, flashed bright. Could it be true?

Julia was trying to read Olivia's face. "Is that not good news?"

Her elation was short lived. "Indeed, it is." But it did not follow that simply because he did not like Miss Manwaring that he would view Olivia, his childhood friend and playmate, as a romantic alternative. Furthermore, she was a female who constantly challenged him, who pushed him to the limits of his temper.

Did *anyone* want such a woman as a wife?

Chapter 16
Jeremy

It had taken more courage to go to Olivia's aunt's house for tea than anything he could remember. All the way back from Worcestershire in the carriage he had argued with himself about the wisdom of making a declaration immediately. Every hour his opinion on the subject vacillated until he could stand it no more and since the hour was favorable when he arrived in the city, he had gone directly to tea, seeking to relieve himself of the suspense that held him captive.

But Olivia was unwell and did not appear, and his impatience buzzed like a swarm of bees who are seeking a new hive. He could barely sit still for the requisite quarter of an hour.

Julia had monopolized him with questions about Miss Manwaring whom she had met in the park. The tone of her questions raised his concerns even more—was Miss Manwaring spreading rumors that he was seeking *her* hand in marriage?

As soon as the time allowed it, he excused himself, sending well wishes via Julia. His agitation had reached critical levels and he needed to burn off some energy.

Mounting his carriage, he requested to be taken to a fencing club. It had been a very long time since he had practiced the sport, but it was just the diversion his restless soul needed.

The grand old building that housed the fencing school was rendered darker by the drizzle that covered London making it feel more like October than June. Large drops fell from leaves that had reached their limit and could no longer hold their watery load. He wiped a fat drop from his nose as he stared up at the Greek revival columns.

At the end of an hour, the instructor pushed back his helmet.

"If I may say so sir, though your technique is lacking, no one could accuse you of a lack of force."

Jeremy pushed his own helmet back and mopped his sweating brow with a clean towel. "I apologize if I have been overly aggressive," he said ruefully. "My life has turned on its head and I am trying to see a way through."

The middle-aged instructor stuck his foil into the ground and placed his hands atop the hilt. "I would wager your distress is over a lady."

Jeremy looked up with surprise.

"I am no mind-reader," he said with a laugh. "But if I had a shilling for every man who has used this sport to clear their minds about problems with the fairer sex, I would be a rich man."

Jeremy lifted his chin. "Is it that obvious?"

"I would rather say after all these years, I'm an expert, sir." He bowed. "Would it be impolitic to ask if you have succeeded in coming to a resolution?"

Several other pairs were sparring around them, and Jeremy glanced at the closest couple, taking a moment to form his answer.

"When one's happiness hinges on the free will of another, there can be no clear resolution before risky declarations are made that lay bare one's heart."

"Oh sir, you have got it bad, if I may say. Most men are here because they are railing against an arranged marriage. Your problem seems to be of actual affection. Does the lady in question return your feelings?"

"That, my dear Brandon, is the crux of the matter. Does she?"

Chapter 17

Olivia

Aunt Frances' neighbor invited them to a card evening and Olivia's mother suggested it was time to withdraw from her self-imposed shell. Since the treachery, Olivia had not been back to scribe for Mr. Manwaring citing ill health, and thankfully, Miss Manwaring had not imposed herself on them for a visit.

Though Olivia now knew that Jeremy was back in London, he had not come to see her. It confirmed her fears that he did not view her as marriage material and that the moment of romantic attention between them had been prompted by her distress.

It had now been several days since her tumble before the queen, and her usually even-tempered mother was becoming irritated. She reminded Olivia that they had put a lot of resources into giving her the best coming out and she was wasting time.

The initial horror that others might gossip about her had dimmed, and it was Julia's last day.

Olivia relented.

Many young, eminently eligible men were in attendance and though Julia flirted with all of them, Olivia could find no enthusiasm for the sport. It was as if her soul was a balloon that was filled with Jeremy and in his absence it deflated.

Toward the middle of the evening, Julia played and sang and was greatly admired. *She* would have no problems when it came time for her presentation at court. Several of the young men abandoned their cards and went to drape themselves around the grand piano.

Though it had filled her with trepidation to enter again into society, it was clear that she had built her fall up into something much greater than it was, as none of the people at the card evening seemed to know anything about it.

The next morning, as she helped Julia into the carriage that would take her home, she felt someone touch her on the shoulder as she waved. Thinking it to be a maid or her mother she turned and was astonished when she came face to face with Jeremy. Though she tried to rein in her emotions, her heart somersaulted, and her stomach danced, but words would not come. For the first time in her life, she was ill at ease in his presence.

"Olivia." Such an expression was on his face but whether it was sorrow or regret she could not tell.

"Jeremy how good it is to see you." Her voice sounded strained and formal to her ears.

He stepped back. "I am sorry to have missed Julia. I saw her when she first came."

"But you have stayed away," she chided with a small smile.

Carriages and people milled past as seconds ticked by. His hand came to his lips then dropped. His head tipped to the side and his shoulders moved.

He had come to tell her bad news, she was sure.

"I—"

"Lord Barclay!" It was Vivienne.

Olivia and Jeremy stared at each other.

"Lord Barclay!" This time louder.

Jeremy turned his head as Vivienne came to claim him by the arm. She cast a smile of triumph at Olivia as she patted Jeremy's forearm with the confidence of ownership.

A dawning comprehension that in spite of what Jeremy had told her sister two days ago, something had changed, and he had come to tell her that he and Miss Manwaring were engaged, emerged like the sun creeping into the dawn sky. Why else would he be so reluctant to talk to her?

She could not bear it.

Avoiding Jeremy's eye, she dipped a curtsey and fled up the stairs and into the house, leaning against the large black door, her chest heaving with wracking sobs.

Chapter 18

Jeremy

Olivia's reaction to his attempt at a declaration, on the pavement outside her aunt's house, baffled Jeremy. In shock at her fleeing, he allowed himself to be maneuvered along the pavement by Miss Manwaring who chattered without stopping, allowing himself the time to replay the recent events in his head.

If Olivia would not have him, perhaps he *should* turn his attentions to Miss Manwaring. She certainly appeared to esteem him, and other successful marriages had been based on less.

"Do you not agree?"

Her perfect face was tilted at a charming angle, but it did not pierce his heart and her constant chattering was frankly, annoying. His face creased into a frown, and she laughed like a cooing bird and tapped his arm with her fan.

"I should guess that you were not listening to me," she said without the least degree of annoyance. "I was asking if you have tried the new teashop just there on the corner."

She pointed to a small shop with lace curtains at the windows and a newly painted sign in black and gold.

In a daze he answered, "I have not, but I am happy to take you."

She cried out with pleasure and dragged him across the cobbles, into the shop that was crowded with young people, sitting around small, round tables covered with lacey tablecloths, containing silver teapots and tiered stands with iced delicacies.

Once they were seated, she grilled him. "Where have you been hiding Lord Barclay?"

"I don't know what you mean."

"Posh! I happen to know you have been back in town for several days, and this is the first time I have spotted you. Anyone would think you were scared of me." She produced a trilling laugh and it struck him in the head like a thousand hornets.

"Can't a man spend time in his own home without raising a scandal of some sort?"

She wagged her finger so close to his nose that his eyes hurt from watching it. "Come, come. It is the season. No one stays home."

He could think of nothing but ridding himself of this cloying woman. "I was tired. Staying up so late is exhausting." He had half a mind to confront her about the rumors, but courtesy prevented him. He must get away or else their appearance together would stoke the flames.

She looked at him sidelong but said, "Will you be going to the Bradshaw's ball tomorrow?"

He would not if it could encourage her delusions. "I have not decided."

"Oh, please come! It will be much more enjoyable if you do. I shall save several sets for you."

A heaviness descended on him. Was this his fate? And now his friendship with Olivia was in peril because of his stupidity.

"I have a secret," she twittered as they waited for their tea.

Nothing she said could hold any interest for him in his current malaise, but manners were indoctrinated into the very fiber of his skin. "Pray, tell me." He hoped the expression he had fashioned projected enthusiasm, even as he searched around for a polite means of escape.

"I believe Stephen is going to ask for Olivia's hand."

He was dumbstruck.

"I thought his ardor had cooled," he protested, his heart thumping nineteen to the dozen. *Because she is lame.*

"So did I, but he has missed her as his scribe and after examining his feelings has decided that he cannot do without her."

"Is that strength enough to secure someone's hand?" he asked.

She opened her fan. "Stephen seems to think so."

It was over. Olivia would never be his. Inside he lost all composure. How he wished he could flee as *she* had.

A maid returned and laid out the tea before them. Vivienne poured. A vision of his future sprung up before his eyes and in panic he looked to the door.

"Here you are. Sugar?"

Was his future life to consist of so mundane conversations? How could he have ever found debates with Olivia exhausting? *This* was exhausting.

His reply was automatic. "Two, please."

"You *are* a sweet tooth. I guessed as much and told my brother so. Stephen, said I, I wager that Lord Barclay has an affection for sugar."

His eyes squinted into a false smile.

"I don't take any. Stephen's research has led him to believe that sugar is responsible for weight gain in women. I take pride in my figure and so from that day forth, I stopped."

His soul screamed for more imaginative discourse. Surely her brother spoke to her about his work from time to time? He took a bite of a pastry and tuned her out as she prattled on and on. He looked at her features in motion and wondered how he had ever thought her attractive. She had good hair, but her nose was too short and her eyes too close together.

"What do you say?" She had placed her chin on a bridge made by her hands, her small reticule dangling against her forearm.

"You must forgive me," he said. "I was thinking of my mother. She has been unwell."

"Oh, my dear, I am so sorry to hear it." She took a sip of her unsweetened tea. "I was asking at what age you think a girl should get married. My brother says for a girl twenty is as good an age as any but for a man he thinks the mid-thirties."

"I beg to differ from your brother. Life can be short. I should not like to defer marriage and the bond it brings, and I should like to have my children while I am young enough to play with and teach them."

Miss Manwaring's eyes widened, and her delicate brows rose. "I am in complete accordance with you."

Jeremy slapped the table. "Indeed, I have suffered from procrastination before. If the perfect woman presents herself then I think it my duty to propose before another suitor beats me to it."

For once, Miss Manwaring was silent, staring straight at him.

A clock struck the hour and she exclaimed, "Good heavens! Is that the time? I have an appointment. But shall we not continue this conversation the next time we meet?"

"If you desire it," he said, completely non-plussed, relieved that he would be rid of her.

Miss Manwaring gulped, gathered her fan and placed a hand on her hat. "I do," she said, and giggled before hurrying out the door.

Jeremy sat staring into space, sick at heart that his hopes and dreams of a happy future lay in tatters at Olivia's feet.

Chapter 19

Olivia

Tonight's event was of much less consequence than Queen Charlotte's ball, and Olivia could find little passion for it. However, she did not want to disappoint her parents and agreed to attend.

The Bradshaw's home was a walled mansion in Kensington, very regular and symmetrical in appearance with torches lighting the avenue.

The ballroom was half the size of that in the palace and Olivia still hoped that no one from that event would remember her. She scanned the room holding her reticule tightly to her chest, nervous as a mouse in an alley full of cats.

Her family found an alcove to sit in and she took the farthest chair, using her mother as a shield, wondering if she would ever live down her clumsiness, watching as other's dance cards were filled by eager young men.

Several dances passed as she watched from the sidelines. She envied the other dancers their healthy legs and then remembered that she had no one to blame for her ailment but herself. She was so caught up in her thoughts that when a masculine voice said her name, she was completely unprepared. Mr. Manwaring stood beside her, dressed very well and looking straight into her face. "I am happy to see that you are feeling better. Might I ask for the next dance. I couldn't help noticing that you were not participating this evening, and I took the risk that your card was not already full."

A strong feeling of righteous indignation began to grow in her stomach and none of the muscles in her face would move. "Why…I…" she stuttered, furious that her mouth would not obey her mind that was screaming at her to refuse the traitor.

"I shall take that as a yes and be back for the next set." He pivoted on his heels and walked away.

Tears of fury stung her eyes. Why did he think he could impose on her in this way? Of course, he did not know that she had heard him at the Queen Charlotte Ball but know it she did. Did he intend to humiliate her further?

"That is kind of Mr. Manwaring, is it not?" her mother asked. "Especially when you have not fulfilled your side of the bargain with regard to the scribing. It portends well for his character I should say."

Olivia did not trust herself to speak and pressed her lips into a thin line.

By the time Mr. Manwaring came to retrieve her, she was trembling with rage. As the dance began, he looked at her, raising his brow. "You are very quiet this evening, Miss Deverell. I am used to being quizzed at the very least."

"I find I have little to say this evening," she replied, hoping the coldness of her answer would convey her displeasure.

"I am truly happy to see that you have recovered. Might I expect you at the house to continue our work? I feel that I am at a critical juncture and your help is imperative if I am to present my findings to the Royal Society before the submission deadline."

The audacity! To slander her in public and then beg her assistance. "I am sure I cannot say."

He ignored her non-committal reply and went on to expound the details of the next portion of his research, and she let the words flow over her without a word of response. When the set came to a close, he asked, "Would you care to take a little air with me?" The doors had been flung open in the midsummer heat and many people milled around in the gardens. He took her silence as acquiescence and offered his arm.

They had not been outside two seconds when he turned to her, his manner all seriousness.

"Miss Deverell—Olivia. I have missed you these past days and have come to a conclusion." He took her hand. "I cannot do without you. Won't you agree to become my wife? We will make a formidable team together."

Stunned was a poor description of the emotions that flooded through her, but outrage prompted her to speech again. She glanced around them to make sure no one could hear what she was about to say.

"Mr. Manwaring," she began through gritted teeth. "You could not have surprised me more had you said that you were preparing an exploration to the moon. The motivation for such a declaration is beyond my significant powers of reasoning to understand since not a week hence I heard you say, with my own ears, that I would not make a suitable wife since I am *lame*." Eyes afire, she locked gazes with him. "What do you say to that?"

She felt satisfaction as the color drained from his face. Then he shook his head. "I did not know that you had heard that pronouncement—it explains why you have not come back to continue as my scribe. But you have misunderstood. Please allow me to explain myself."

She placed her hands on her hips and scowled.

"I can appreciate how it sounded and I apologize for what must have seemed like heaping coals on an already difficult situation. But you must believe me when I say that I was trying to dissuade a group of very eager suitors. I made that comment in the hopes of preventing them from pursuing you. I had already decided to ask for your hand and wanted to clear the field."

His face creased with regret and her heart softened.

"I know I am not the finest looking gentleman. I was afraid that if you received other, more favorable offers, that

100

I would have no hope of succeeding. I am only sorry that you heard it. It was badly done, and I am ashamed."

His shoulders slumped and his head hung in apparent remorse. His confession took the wind right out of her sails.

"How could you disparage me so?" she asked, her tone imploring. "I have a slight limp from a childhood injury that aches when I use it too much. How do you expect me to accept a man who considers me a cripple?"

"I never used that offensive phrase!" he said with passion. "I swear that was not my intent." A whiff of desperation surrounded his words. "Truly! I only said it to dissuade others. Improve my own chances."

"Do you love me?" she demanded.

"I have never had such a connection to a woman as I have felt when sharing my work with you. I did not think there was a woman on the planet who was my equal in such things. Is not that love?"

As she listened to his protestations, Olivia's mind was in chaos. She considered the way she had felt since realizing she loved Jeremy. Mr. Manwaring's description of his sentiments for her did not come close to the poetry of her affection for Jeremy. But if he was to be engaged to another? The playing field had changed. With Jeremy out of reach, should she say yes to Mr. Manwaring? She knew that she would never experience the same depth of emotion for him, and she doubted that what he felt for her was love. It would be a working relationship and once the children came, she would have to choose between following Mr. Manwaring on his excursions or staying behind with them. It was not a choice she wanted to make. He might give her credit when his star rose, but what would she be required to sacrifice? And now that her heart knew what true love was, she could not settle for second best, even if it meant not marrying at all.

His vulnerability swayed her, but she had to refuse. "I am flattered by your proposal…"

"But..." he added, his face etched with concern.

"But regretfully, I cannot accept. I am not sure that what you feel for me is love—perhaps a happy companionship, but not love." He began to interrupt but she lifted her palm to stop him. "Before I met you, I thought that all I wanted was to travel the world and discover and learn in my own right or at least share the journey of discovery with another. But since then, I have had experiences that have changed me. I believe I can realize the same satisfaction from reading about such things in books and discussing them with my sisters. And though I like you and appreciate the opportunities you have offered me, I do not love you. You deserve someone who does. And so do I."

The look of disappointment in his eyes tore at her heart.

"Perhaps given a little more time?" he pleaded.

She shook her head and pursed her lips. "I am sorry."

There was no anger, no insults hurled that she was making the biggest mistake of her life, no recriminations— and for that she was grateful.

He left quietly, and she sank to a stone bench as the music from the ballroom scattered across the star-lit gardens. It had drained her to hear his proposal and refuse him. She wanted nothing more than to curl into a ball and take a restorative nap on the bench. Instead, she waited ten minutes and then went in search of her family hoping that she might persuade them to leave.

Her season had come to a close and she had failed her sisters.

Chapter 20
Jeremy

Jeremy was in further need of distraction and had gone to an old school friend's house to get lost in some archery. Several other young men in need of diversion from so much formal eating, drinking, and dancing had also arrived to enjoy a lazy afternoon. They had all done two rounds and were resting under a large oak with some lemonade when one of the men, a stranger to Jeremy, said, "Do any of you happen to know Stephen Manwaring?"

Jeremy's arm was hanging over the edge of a wicker chair, his fingers stroking the lush, green grass. He had no intention of admitting to knowing Manwaring. He had still not forgiven him for offending Olivia so publicly.

"No," said the host, and several others murmured similarly. "I've heard *of* him, of course. Who hasn't?"

"Indeed," said the first. "Well, there are rumors all over town that he is on the brink of getting married."

Jeremy shot to an upright position.

"To whom?" asked the host.

"Some country bumpkin who set her cap at him. Quite the intellectual they say. Sounds like a match made in heaven, though I would wager she will cramp his explorations. She might share his enthusiasm for academics but when the little ones come, she won't want him traipsing all over creation for months at a time, you mark my words."

What? The last he knew, Olivia was angry with Stephen for insulting her in public. Had there been a reconciliation?

"Has he asked?" said a chap prone on the lawn, his hat shielding his face from the sun. "There is always time to dissuade him!" He laughed lazily.

A cold hand clutched Jeremy's heart and his breath stalled in his chest. This is exactly what Olivia had been originally hoping for in coming to London. And now it appeared the deed was done.

He was too late!

Had he gone to her aunt's house today, instead of running away, he likely would have learned the news for himself and felt heart sick at the idea of having to endure the celebrations.

"Winston!" cried the host as a newcomer approached the group. "What the devil have you been doing? You have missed two rounds already!"

"I had a late night and no one woke me this morning. Slept right through breakfast and lunch but I'm here now."

"What kept you up so late?" asked the host.

"I was at Bradshaw's ball playing cards when a chap burst in to tell us that one of the debutantes had refused Stephen Manwaring."

"Refused him?" shouted Jeremy. "Are you sure?"

"I am more than sure. I heard it from the great man himself. He came to play but had lost his spirit and left to go home."

Jeremy excused himself, grabbed his jacket, and shoved his feet back into his boots.

"Where are *you* going?" asked the host.

"To seek my fortune!" he cried as he ran over the lawn, waving behind him.

Chapter 21

Olivia

Surrounded by opulent crimson taffeta on the walls and delicate French furniture, Olivia was begging her mother to leave London.

"Mama, I am so grateful for all the opportunities you have offered me, and I *have* been presented at court and made the rounds. If any young man wants to pursue me, he can find out where I live. But I have tired of the social whirl, and I am ready to go back to Worcester Park. *Please,* let us go home."

The lines on her mother's face betrayed her frustration. "I just don't understand, Olivia. We have made all this effort to give you a proper season as becomes a young gentlewoman, and you want to cut it short. This does not resemble appreciation."

"I do appreciate it! I do!" she responded. "But I am weary of it all, and my ankle has weakened—it cannot take any more balls."

She draped her arms around her mother's neck. "It has been wonderful, and you will never know how obliged to you I am for this experience and the people I have met, but one can have too much of a good thing." She kissed her mother's cheek.

The door to her mother's bedchamber flew open and Aunt Frances stood panting from her recent flight up the stairs.

"She refused him, sister," declared her aunt.

Mrs. Deverell looked from her sister to her child and back again. "Who refused whom, Frances?"

Aunt Frances pointed a parasol at Olivia who cringed. "Olivia refused Mr. Stephen Manwaring. It is all over town."

Mrs. Deverell's face tightened. "Is this true, child?"

Olivia dropped her eyes to the floor, wishing a great hole would open up and swallow her whole. "It is."

"Heavens! Why did you not tell me?" Her voice did not hold the hint of accusation that her aunt's did.

"Because I do not love him, and he only saw me as a scribe—not as a woman. Not as a wife."

Aunt Frances stood by the door, enraptured by the unfolding drama.

"Come, sit," said her mother gently, reminding Olivia of times when she was a child. "Frances, let me have some time alone with Olivia." Aunt Frances huffed, and with eyes squinted and lower lip jutting out, left the room.

"Now, tell me everything," said her mother.

Olivia explained what had happened at the Queen Charlotte Ball when she had heard Manwaring blatantly disparage her to her male peers. Mrs. Deverell reached for her hand. "This is the true reason you want to leave, is it not?"

"Yes." *And the fact that Jeremy is to propose to Miss Manwaring and I cannot bear to be here for it.*

"Now I understand." Her mother tapped her chin. "Leaving two weeks early will not be noticed, I daresay. Let me talk to your father."

Olivia had never loved her mother more.

As they journeyed back to Worcester Park, she could not bring herself to talk but sat staring out the window as her parents were rocked to sleep.

Miserable at heart, Olivia allowed her thoughts free rein to condemn her. How could she have been blind to the fine man Jeremy had become? And now she would have to feign happiness that Vivienne would be mistress of his great estate. The very thought was like a gall of bitterness and though she loved her family home to distraction, she devised all sorts of plans that involved moving away from Worcester Park after Jeremy's marriage.

It took all her might to strain against the tears as they bumped along but as soon as they reached her beloved house, she ran up the stairs with abandon to indulge, hoping that the tears would purge her sorrow.

Chapter 22
Jeremy

Having rushed home to bathe and change, Jeremy appeared at Aunt Frances's townhome, excited as a schoolboy at Christmas. His breast was full of renewed hope and an intention to explain all his feelings to Olivia.

"My dear Lord Barclay," crooned Aunt Frances, "they left this morning." Her eyes were bulging with gossip, but her breeding prevented her from spilling the intelligence. "Did they not leave a message for you to that effect? I *know* how close your families are." She narrowed her eyes at him.

"They did not," he responded, backing out of the room. "But I hope you will accept my apologies for not staying this afternoon."

"Of course," said Aunt Frances, watching him as a cat might watch a bird.

He promptly left the salon and bounding down the steps, ran straight into Miss Manwaring.

"I beg your pardon," he said, clutching his hat and holding Miss Manwaring up by the elbow as she wobbled on the steps. "But I must leave this instant."

"Surely not!" she remonstrated. "I stopped by your townhome and was told I might find you here. I was hoping to continue our conversation from the other day." She tipped her head to the side and blinked a dozen times.

"My dear Miss Manwaring," he began, and a tiny smile played along her lips. "I do hope that I am not guilty of leading you to misunderstand my intentions."

The small smile flattened.

"It was not deliberately done, I assure you, but I must tell you that my heart is already taken. I plan to make a play for the woman I love—the woman I have always loved.

Miss Manwaring jutted out her bottom lip and squinted. "I should say, sir, that you have, indeed, misled me. What was all that talk of marriage? What was a girl supposed to think?"

She stamped her foot and rearranged the reticule on her arm. "I believe your very words were, '*I would think it my duty to propose before another suitor beats me to it.*' That is tantamount to a declaration."

"I hate to contradict a member of the opposite sex, but you were the one who brought up the topic. I was merely responding to your comment. I am sorry if my meaning was misinterpreted but I can assure you it was not intentional." He took a step back from her wrath. "I am leaving London this instant. I have had enough of the season for one year."

The eyes he had once thought pretty were marred by fury. "That is all you have to say? I might defame you for breach of contract, sir."

His laugh sounded hollow and desperate in his ears. He had to get away. "There is no contract to be breached."

Her delicate face turned ugly with a scowl. "That is what *you* say. I have told others that I expected a proposal very soon. Now I shall be disgraced."

"I am very sorry for it, but I made no such declaration. I bid you good day." He swept his hat from his head as Miss Manwaring stared at him, her angry mouth twisted.

"I must go!" he cried behind him, practically running down the street.

Standing at the base of the old, tall oak tree, he could just make out her flat, white shoe and the bottom of her petticoats.

And sniffing.

He knew that she was totally unaware of his presence and that she believed him to be still in town.

"I have come to the conclusion that Descartes is a fool," he declared loudly.

A gasp from above made him smile.

Her soggy voice drifted down from above. "How dare you disparage the reputation of so fine a scholar!"

Arms akimbo, he said, "Then I beg you would come down and defend him to my face."

"I cannot. I am rather sad today and not up to debating." Her voice was weak and wobbly.

He tried to look up farther, to catch a glimpse of her dear face. "Sad? And what, pray, do you have to be sad about?"

"I have been a fool."

"That is not unusual." He waited for a retort.

She ignored his inflammatory comment. "Did Miss Manwaring come with you? I send down my congratulations."

"Why would Miss Manwaring come with me, and why do you need to send congratulations? Did I win a prize of some kind?"

"Don't be obtuse, Jeremy," she said languidly. "It does not become you. You know very well I am talking of your engagement."

He closed his eyes and took in a deep, happy breath.

"I am not engaged, Olivia."

Another gasp made its way down the tree. "But you will soon propose to her, will you not?"

A smile tugged at his lips. "Now why would I propose to someone I do not care for?"

The sound of ripping fabric preceded Olivia's descent as she slipped the last few feet and landed in a heap at his feet.

"You do not love Miss Manwaring?" she asked, looking up from the pile of petticoats.

He pulled her to her feet so that they stood face to face. "I do not. But there is another I do love, and I have come to tell you."

Tears pooled in her eyes, and he fought the urge to kiss them away.

"Another? What is her name?"

"I think you know." He reached a hand to cup her cheek.

Her bottom lip trembled. "I do not."

He leaned forward and her eyes widened. Those beloved, cornflower blue eyes he had seen almost every day of his life. He hesitated, drinking in the anticipation of a kiss he had only dreamed of for several years. Her pupils enlarged, reflecting his own eyes like a mirror. She blinked and her thick, dark lashes swept a tear over her lid. He reached up to brush it with his thumb and felt her shiver beneath his skin. Every inch of him ached to kiss those lips. She dropped her gaze to his mouth, inviting him, and a wave of yearning filled his whole body. He closed the gap as her eyes closed and gently brushed her lips with his own, igniting a flame that had simmered in his heart for a long time. She tasted like summer and fresh lemonade and he surrendered utterly, allowing her to pull him under as she responded to his kiss.

She finally pulled away and laid her head against his chest, melting into him.

"I thought I had lost you," he began, pushing her errant curls from her forehead. "I heard that Stephen Manwaring was preparing to propose and imagined that you would forgive him for ridiculing you and jump at the chance for acceptance into his world of academics and science."

"I did forgive him," she confessed. "But I do not love him, and the learning was not enough. He did not love me either." She looked up at him through wet lashes. "And besides, I had finally realized it was you I loved. Who I have always loved. But I thought it was too late and I had to run away." She smiled. "But what about you and Miss Manwaring?"

"It was all one-sided. I think she was interested in my title." He chuckled and ran a finger across her chin. "It has always been you, Olivia. I was just waiting and hoping that you would discover the same. When I heard that he had proposed, I was frantic. I learned of your refusal by chance and rushed to see you at your aunt's house but you had gone."

She looked down. "Yes. I could not face being in town and hearing of your upcoming nuptials. When you found me in the tree, I had been devising schemes to move away, in fact."

He laughed, reaching for the hands he had longed to hold, lacing his fingers through hers. Putting them to his lips, he glanced up, thrilled to see heat in her expression. Disengaging his hands, he wrapped her in his arms, drunk on the scent of her hair.

But he still had unfinished business.

He stepped back and she whimpered, but as he knelt down on one knee, she covered her mouth with her palms, her azure eyes blazing with joy. He held out a hand and she took it.

"Olivia Deverell, will you make me the happiest man on earth and consent to be my wife?"

"Only if you will agree to consider Mr. Descartes' position on innate intelligence."

He pulled her down, taking her face in his hands and pressing his mouth softly to hers. She responded.

"I expect we can come to some agreement," he whispered against her lips.

The End

I hope you enjoyed the first book of the *Women of Worcester* series, *Olivia*. Book two, *Julia*, is also available.

Julia - https://amzn.to/384MkR7

Julia Deverell is a talented musician with a secret. Alexander Trevellyan threatens to expose that secret. Can they come to some agreement? Will they fall in love in the process?

When Julia Deverell plays the piano, everyone is entranced, even the handsome stranger who guesses her secret. But when she hears that he has criticized her method in public she declares him public enemy number one. However, when circumstances force them together, she cannot deny he possesses an undeniable charisma. If only she had not determined to dislike him.

Alex is a classical music student at Oxford. Music is not one of the approved careers for second sons and he endures lifelong ridicule, but his exceptional talent dictates the future course of his life. When he attends his aunt's party and hears Julia play, he is mesmerized until she makes an error and he guesses her secret. Envy drives him to criticize her in the hearing of another guest but almost immediately he regrets his action and vows never to let petty jealousy get the better of him again.

When asked to play a duet with Julia by his aunt, an irrefutable attraction sparks but Julia seems determined to ignore it and shun him. Can he convince her to give him a chance?

Julia is the second novella in the Women of Worcester series.

If you would like to read my other romances - *The Governess of Banbury Park, The Secret of Haversham House, Misfortune is a Rolling Tide* go to:

The Governess of Banbury Park -
https://amzn.to/3dy3CVG

She is suddenly penniless and alone. He is dashing and well-connected. Can he save her?

At the reading of her father's will, Sophia Cavanaugh learns that she is destitute. Impoverished, grief-stricken and alone in the world, she sees only one course open to her—becoming a governess. With little experience and no references, securing a position proves more difficult than expected until she finds a champion in the dashing Charles Mortimer. He quickly captures her heart but are the feelings mutual?

Charles's meddling mother provides Sophia a position and the two are parted, but fate throws them back together. Will Sophia risk her heart and confess her love before it is too late?

The Secret of Haversham House -
https://amzn.to/3dy3WUo

EIGHTEEN-YEAR-OLD FRANCESCA HAVERSHAM is privileged, beautiful, and naïve. Lineage, titles, and wealth are the ultimate virtues among nineteenth-century English aristocracy, and Francesca is elite society's newest and most celebrated debutante from one of England's most illustrious families. Her pedigree is impeccable—or is it?

HER COMING-OUT BALL brings with it the appearance of one Mr. Langley Ashbourne, and Francesca is immediately taken in by his handsome features and flattering words. But not everything is as it seems, and flowery comments can only hide dark truths for so long. Meanwhile, a long-buried secret creeps ever closer to the light, one that would destroy her comfortable life, tarnish her family's character, and ruin all hopes of a reputable marriage.

Misfortune is a Rolling Tide -
https://amzn.to/3tJDZtk

An unforgettable novel that sweeps the reader from the depths of the English countryside to the beauties of Florence, Italy. and on to the primitive shores of the emerging colony of Australia.

At the turn of the nineteenth century, the expectations of the young are often dependent on the whims of the adults who guide them. Such is the sad case of Charlotte Abernathy and Henry Westbrook. Throw in an eccentric, wealthy maiden aunt whose life is stuck in the era of the French Revolution, and you have a recipe for disaster. Forces conspire against the couple and Charlotte is forced into an arranged marriage with an absent-minded intellectual. In desperation, Henry recklessly signs up for a dangerous military mission to Australia where he barely escapes with his life.

Circumstances come full circle and the treachery behind their misfortunes is exposed. But it is all too late as Charlotte's marriage forever divides them.

This is a tale of lost expectations, heartbreak and redemption whose enduring characters will stay with the reader long after the book is finished.

To learn more about Julie and her current projects go to her website: www.juliematern.com

Go to this link: https://dl.bookfunnel.com/m6bdpy27u8 to subscribe to her newsletter and receive a free Christmas Regency Romance novella.

You can also follow her on Facebook at: https://www.facebook.com/juliematernauthor

About the Author

Born and raised in England, Julie Matern has bounced all around America with her husband and their family. At a crossroads, she decided to try her hand at writing before going back to work as a teacher. After a foray into children's historical fiction, a love for all things Jane Austen led to trying her hand at Regency Romance. She was smitten. Olivia is the fourth book in that genre.

She now lives in Utah, at the foot of a mountain range whose views give her inspiration.

Acknowledgements

My editor Jolene Perry of Waypoint Author Academy.
Sending my work to editors is the most terrifying part of
the process for me but Jolene offers correction and
constructive criticism without crushing my fragile ego.

My cheerleader, marketer and IT guy – Todd Matern
A lot of the time during the marketing side of being an
author I am running around with my hair on fire. Todd is
the yin to my yang. He calms me down and takes over
when I am yelling at the computer.

My beta readers – Francesca Matern, Stina Van Cott,
Your reactions to my characters and plot are invaluable.

My proofreader Tammy.

Printed in Great Britain
by Amazon

22872130R00069